Real Science-4-Kids

Teacher's Manual

Level I

Dr. R. W. Keller

CHEMISTRY Biology PHYSICS

RealScience 4 Kids

Cover design: David Keller
Opening page: David Keller, Rebecca Keller
Illustrations: Rebecca Keller

Copyright © 2004, 2005, 2007 Gravitas Publications, Inc.

Real Science-4-Kids: Combined Teacher's Manual Level I

ISBN 0-9749149-6-7
ISBN 13: 9780974914961

Published by Gravitas Publications, Inc.
P.O. Box 4790
Albuquerque, NM 87196-4790

Printed in USA

GRAVITAS
PUBLICATIONS INC

A note from the author

This curriculum is designed to give students both solid science information and hands-on experimentation. This level is geared towards fourth through sixth grades, but much of the information in the text is very different from what is taught at this grade level in other textbooks. I feel that students beginning in the fourth grade can grasp most of the concepts presented here. This is a *real* science text, so scientific terms are used throughout. It is not important at this time for the students to master the terminology, but it *is* important that they be exposed to the real terms used to describe science.

Each chapter has two parts: a reading part and an experimental part. In the teacher's text, an estimate is given for the time needed to complete each chapter. It is not important that both the reading portion and the experimental portion be conducted in a single sitting. It may be better to split these into two separate days, depending on the interest level of the child and the energy level of the teacher. Also, questions not addressed in the teacher's manual may arise, and extra time may be required to investigate these questions before proceeding with the experimental section.

Each experiment is a *real* science experiment and not just a demonstration. These are designed to engage the students in an actual scientific investigation. The experiments are simple, but they are written the way real scientists actually perform experiments in the laboratory. With this foundation, it is my hope that the students will eventually begin to think of their own experiments and test their own ideas scientifically.

Enjoy!
R. W. Keller

How to use this manual

This teacher's manual provides additional information and answers to the laboratory experiments and review pages for Chemistry, Biology, and Physics. The additional information for each chapter is provided as supplementary material in case questions arise while reading the text. It is not necessary for the students to learn this additional material as most of it is beyond the scope of this level. However, the teacher may find it useful for answering questions.

The laboratory section (or Experiments) together with the Review are found at the end of each chapter. All of the experiments have been tested, but it is not unusual for an experiment to fail. Usually, repeating an experiment helps both student and teacher see where an error may have been made. However, not all repeated experiments work either. Do not worry if an experiment fails. Encourage the student to troubleshoot and investigate possible errors.

Getting started

The easiest way to follow this curriculum is to have all of the materials needed for each lesson ready before you begin. A small shelf or cupboard or even a plastic bin can be dedicated to holding most of the necessary chemicals and equipment. Those items that need to be fresh are indicated at the beginning of each lesson. The following is a partial list of chemicals and equipment required for the experiments. The items are divided into the following categories; Provided items, Grocery store items, and Speciality store items.

Provided items
Periodic table of elements (Chemistry Level I text)

Common household items
pennies
metal can open at both ends (any regular sized food can open at both ends)
cardboard tube [such as a wrapping paper tube]
paper (white copy paper)

Grocery store items
several small jars (baby food jars)
two large glass jars (pickle or mayonnaise jar)
white vinegar
balsamic vinegar
baking soda
measuring spoons
eye droppers
Elmer's white glue
Elmer's blue glue
liquid laundry starch (or Borax)
popsicle sticks
distilled water
coffee filters
ammonia
rubbing alcohol
paper towels
coffee filters
bleach
sugar
salt
food coloring
dish soap
wax paper
rubber bands

paper clips

ruler

tacks or straight pins

aluminum foil

balloons

batteries [1.5 Volts, any size]

toothpicks

Specialty store items

marking pens for writing on glass or wax paper

iodine (Walgreen's or other pharmacy store)

ball point ink pens of various colors (art store)

timer or stop watch (Radio Shack)

balance, food scale, mail scale (Office Max)

marbles of different sizes (toy store)

plastic-coated copper wire (Home Depot)

duct tape [or other strong tape]

plastic or rubber rod (toy store)

silk fabric (fabric store)

small magnets (toy store)

iron filings (educational supply store or can be collected from outdoor dirt, see Section 8.2)

electrical wire (Home Depot)

small light bulb/socket kit (Home Depot)

electrical tape (Home Depot)

metal rod (such as a long screwdriver)

glass or plastic prism (Educational supply store)

flashlight (Radio Shack)

laser pointer (Radio Shack)

long wooden craft stick (art supply store)

Several experiments require living organisms. Some of these can be found in the backyard or local environment. Some living things may also be purchased from a local pet store. If necessary, all of the living things can be purchased from internet sources. Wards Natural Science company is a recommended source for all experiments with living things or needing extra equipment not found in the kitchen pantry.

Ward's Natural Science: www.wardsci.com

Laboratory safety

Most of these experiments use household items. However, some items, such as iodine, are extremely poisonous. Extra care should be taken while working with all chemicals in this series of experiments. The following are some general laboratory precautions that should be applied to the home laboratory:

- Never put things in your mouth unless the experiment tells you to. This means that food items should not be eaten unless it is part of the experiment.

- Use safety glasses while using glass objects or strong chemicals such as bleach.

- Wash hands after handling all chemicals.

- Use adult supervision while working with iodine or glassware and when conductiong any step requiring a stove.

Contents

PHYSICS

CHEMISTRY

Materials at a glance

Experiment 1	Experiment 2	Experiment 3	Experiment 4	Experiment 5	Experiment 6	Experiment 7	Experiment 8	Experiment 9	Experiment 10
pen paper food labels dictionary encyclopedia Periodic table of elements	toothpicks small marshmallows large marshmallows	baking soda lemon juice balsamic vinegar sugar salt egg whites (or milk) several small jars eye dropper	1/2 head red cabbage distilled water small jars coffee filters eye dropper ammonia vinegar soda pop milk mineral water	red cabbage indicator (Exp. 4) ammonia vinegar small jars measuring spoons	vinegar rubbing alcohol ammonia vegetable oil melted butter small jars food coloring dish soap	multi-colored ink pen black ink pen rubbing alcohol coffee filters (white) small jars	iodine food items: pasta, bread, celery, banana, potato, apple liquid laundry starch white paper eye dropper	liquid laundry starch (or Borax) Elmer's white glue Elmer's blue glue small jars marker popsicle stick for stirring	iodine bread timer wax paper marking pen

Chapter 1: Matter

Time Required:

> Text reading - 30 minutes
> Experimental - 1 hour

Experimental setup:

> NONE

Additional Materials:

> dictionary
> encyclopedia
> food labels

Overall Objectives:

This chapter will introduce the concept that all things, living and nonliving, are made of the same fundamental components called atoms. It is important to help the students understand that although the world is full of a large number of both living and nonliving things, there is only a limited number of atoms, or elements, that make up all things. The variety observed in all things is a result of the vast number of ways that atoms can be combined with one another. For example, sodium (Na) is found in table salt together with chlorine (Cl) to make "sodium chloride" (NaCl). However, if you add an oxygen atom (O) and make "sodium hypochlorite," NaOCl, you get bleach.

1.1 Introduction

Matter is a general term for describing what all things are made of.

Chemistry is that area of science mainly concerned with the way atoms combine to form chemical bonds.

There are several different subdisciplines within chemistry:

Physical chemistry is concerned with the fundamental physics of atoms.

Biochemistry is concerned with matter from living things.

Organic chemistry is concerned with the chemistry of carbon (C) containing compounds.

Analytical chemistry deals with analyzing the composition of matter.

Inorganic chemistry is concerned with mostly noncarbon compounds.

1.2 Atoms

The students will be introduced to the following terms:

Atoms
Protons
Neutrons
Electrons

Atoms, protons, neutrons and electrons are more specific terms for matter.

Atoms are very small and cannot be seen by the naked eye. If an atom were the size of a tennis ball, the average man (6 ft. tall) would stand one million kilometers high — almost the distance from here to the sun.

Protons and neutrons are roughly equal in size and both have an atomic mass of 1 amu (atomic mass unit). A proton carries a positive charge and a neutron carries no charge; it is neutral. By comparison, the electron is 1/1836 of the mass of a proton. The electron carries a negative charge that is equal in magnitude to the charge on a proton. For neutral atoms, the number of electrons equals the number of protons. The number of neutrons does not always equal the number of protons or electrons in neutral atoms.

The nucleus contains the protons and neutrons and is much smaller than the full atom. Most of the volume of an atom is occupied by the electrons.

The space occupied by the electrons surrounds the proton-neutron core and is called an orbital or electron cloud. Orbitals can have a variety of shapes, which the students will learn later on. The different shapes of electron clouds are very important for understanding how atoms combine with each other.

1.3 Periodic Table

The periodic table of elements is a large chart that organizes and categorizes all of the elements according to their chemical properties.

The periodic table illustrates the general law of periodicity among all of the elements. This means that certain chemical properties of the atoms repeat. For example, fluorine (F) undergoes similar chemical reactions as chlorine (Cl), bromine (Br), iodine (I), and astatine (As). All of these similar elements are arranged in a single column of the periodic table. Grouping the elements according to their chemical properties gives rise to the "periods" which are the horizontal rows.

There are three short periods of 2, 8, and 8 elements:

hydrogen -> helium   [period of 2 elements]
lithium -> neon [period of 8 elements]
sodium -> argon [period of 8 elements]

and then three longer periods of 18, 18, and 32:

potassium -> krypton [period of 18 elements]
rubidium ->xenon [period of 18 elements]
cesium ->radon [period of 32 elements]

The last period is predicted to contain 32 elements, but notice that the number of elements stops at 112.

The last naturally occurring element is uranium at 92 protons. the elements after uranium are artificially made.

The symbols of elements are not always the same as the first letter of the English name since some elements were named in other languages. Some examples are given in the student text.

Page 5 of the student text gives a brief explanation for some of the details in the periodic table.

The number in the upper-left-hand corner of each element square is the atomic number. This number tells how many protons the atom contains. The atomic number is not always in the upper-left-hand corner of the block representing each element: it can be in the middle or on the right.

The number below the name is the atomic weight. The atomic weight is the sum of the weight of the protons, neutrons, and electrons. Because the electrons have essentially no mass, the atomic weight can be considered to be the sum of just the weight for the protons and neutrons. Because protons and neutrons are essentially "1 atomic mass unit" each, the number of neutrons can be determined by subtracting the atomic number from the atomic weight.

Example: Hydrogen has an atomic number of 1. This means that hydrogen has one proton. Hydrogen has an atomic weight close to one, which means that all of the weight is due to the single proton. There are no neutrons.

Another example is uranium:

> number of protons: 92
> atomic weight: 238
> number of neutrons: 238 minus 92 = 146

NOTE:

Although the atomic weight is actually 238.0289, it can be rounded to 238 to calculate the number of neutrons.

Vertically, the elements are organized according to similar chemical properties.

The elements on the far right of the periodic table are the noble gases. The noble gases do not react with other elements in general. It is possible to get some of the noble gases to react, but it is very difficult. The noble gases are always found in nature as single atoms and not in pairs like other gases such as oxygen and nitrogen.

The elements on the far left are called the alkali metals. These elements are very reactive. Lithium (Li), sodium (Na), and potassium (K) react very violently with water. They also form salts with the halogens, which form the column next to the noble gases. Some common salts include sodium chloride (NaCl), lithium chloride (LiCl), potassium chloride (KCl). Sodium chloride (NaCl) is common table salt. Potassium chloride (KCl) is a table salt alternative that is used by many people with high blood pressure.

There are other "trends" or properties that are illustrated with the periodic table, such as atomic size and electronegativity, but these will be introduced later.

The most important points to emphasize with the periodic table are the following:

- All of the elements that make up all things, living and nonliving, are on the periodic table.

- The periodic table illustrates an underlying order or "periodicity" among all of the elements.

- Mendeleev discovered the overall order of elements through scientific investigation and assembled the first periodic table.

1.4 Summary

Discuss with the students the main points of this chapter.

- Point out that everything we can touch is made of atoms. Have the students name several different items and discuss how these items are all made of atoms.

- Review that atoms are made of smaller particles called protons, neutrons, and electrons. Protons and neutrons are together in the atomic core, and electrons are found in the electron cloud surrounding the core.

- Review that the number of protons equals the number of electrons in an atom. This is true for neutral atoms. It is possible to remove an electron from an atom or add an electron to an atom. The atom is called an ion in this case. However, this is beyond the scope of this level.

- All of the elements known are found on the periodic table of elements. New elements can be made by man-made means, but all naturally occuring elements are already known.

- Review that all elements are in groups that are similar. For example, the noble gases behave alike and are in the same column.

NOTES:

Experiment 1:   What is it made of?   Date:

Objective:

To become familiar with the periodic table of elements and investigate the composition of some common items.

Materials:

pen
paper
food labels
dictionary
encyclopedia
Periodic Table of Elements

Directions:

1. Take out the periodic table of elements and answer the following questions:

   A. How many protons does aluminum have? How many electrons?

   B. What is the symbol for carbon?

   C. List all of the elements that have chemical properties similar to helium.

   D. What is the atomic weight for nitrogen? How many neutrons does nitrogen have?

2. Next, think of several different items and write them in the column labeled "Item." These can be any item, like "tires" or "cereal." Try to be specific. For example, instead of writing just "cereal," write "corn cereal" or "sweet colored cereal."

3. Next look up in an encyclopedia or on the food label the composition of the items you have selected. Try to be as specific as possible while identifying the composition. For example, if your cereal contains vitamin C, write "sodium ascorbate" if that name is also listed. Try to identify any elements in the compounds you have listed. For example, vitamin C contains the element "sodium."

4. Write the source next to the composition. "Source" means where you got your information, for example, "food label" or "encyclopedia."

The goals of this experiment are to help the students begin to investigate the things in their world and to have them examine what those things are made of.

There are many "right" answers for this experiment, and the elemental composition will not be available for all items from basic resources such as the dictionary or encyclopedia. For example,

Things made of metals:

soda cans and aluminum foil - aluminum
silverware (steel) - iron, nickel, silver
coins - copper, nickel
jewelry - gold, silver

Things we eat:

salt - sodium and chlorine
sugar - carbon, oxygen, hydrogen
water - hydrogen and oxygen
bread (carbohydrates) - carbon, oxygen, hydrogen, and other proteins and things.

Also, students can select food items with labels such as cake mixes, cereal, noodles, and vitamins (with vitamins the label is very detailed and the students can also find out how much of something is in the vitamin).

NOTE:
The students DO NOT need to find out every component for each item. To say that cake mix contains salt, flour, and sugar is enough. Let the students go as far as they want with a particular item. Also, it is not necessary to look up components for each item given. Pick a few and go from there.

Sample Answers to Questions:

A. *Aluminum has 13 protons. Aluminum also has 13 electrons.*

B. *The symbol for carbon is "C."*

C. *The elements that have the same chemical properties as helium are neon, argon, krypton xenon, and radon.*

D. *The atomic weight for nitrogen is 14.0067. Nitrogen has 7 neutrons.*

Item	Composition	Source
car tires	*rubber (carbon and hydrogen)*	*Webster's Dictionary , page 1582*
graham crackers	*sodium bicarbonate (sodium)*	*food label*
graham crackers	*salt (sodium, chlorine)*	*food label, dictionary, page 1600*

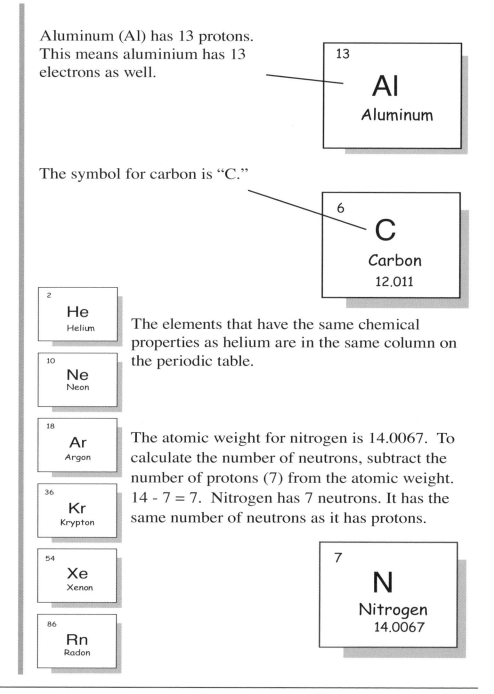

Aluminum (Al) has 13 protons. This means aluminium has 13 electrons as well.

13
Al
Aluminum

The symbol for carbon is "C."

6
C
Carbon
12.011

2
He
Helium

10
Ne
Neon

18
Ar
Argon

36
Kr
Krypton

54
Xe
Xenon

86
Rn
Radon

The elements that have the same chemical properties as helium are in the same column on the periodic table.

The atomic weight for nitrogen is 14.0067. To calculate the number of neutrons, subtract the number of protons (7) from the atomic weight. 14 - 7 = 7. Nitrogen has 7 neutrons. It has the same number of neutrons as it has protons.

7
N
Nitrogen
14.0067

Results:

Briefly describe what you discovered about the composition of the various items.

For example,

Kellogg's Sugar Smacks™ cereal contains vitamin C which is called sodium ascorbate.

Table salt is made of sodium and chlorine.

Iodized table salt contains sodium, chlorine, and iodine.

Chocolate cake mix contains sugar.

Sugar has oxygen, hydrogen ,and carbon in it.

Conclusions:

State here what "conclusions" can be made.

For example,

Many cereals contain sodium in the form of salt and vitamin C.

Some peanut butter contains sugar.

Rubber contains carbon and hydrogen.

Help the students write accurate statements about the data they have collected.

Some examples are given.

Help the students think specifically about what their data show. This is an important critical thinking step that will help them evaluate future experiments.

Try to help them write concluding statements that are valid. Encourage them to avoid stating options or anything that cannot be drawn strictly from their data.

For example, it may be true that all cereals contain "salt." However, this particular investigation cannot confirm or deny that conclusion. The most that can be stated from this investigation is "Brand X contains salt, and Brand Y contains salt" but any further statement is conjecture.

Help them formulate their conclusions using the words *some*, *all*, *many* and *none*. Point out that the statement, "All cereals contain salt" is not valid, but based on this investigation it is valid to say, "Some cereals contain salt."

Again, there are numerous "right" answers. One student may list "sugar" as a component in soup, and another may list "salt," and both could be "right." The true test is wheteher the statements about the data are valid or not valid.

Also, try to show them where broad statements can be made accordingly. For example, "All U.S. pennies contain copper" is probably a valid statement even though we haven't checked every U.S. penny.

This may seem fairly subtle, but the main point is to help them understand the kinds of valid conclusions science can offer based on scientific investigation.

Review

Define the following terms:

chemistry	*A branch of science concerned with the properties of matter.*
matter	*A general term for what makes up all things.*
atoms (atomos)	*The fundamental building blocks of matter. Atomos is a Greek word that means uncuttable.*
proton	*A small particle found inside atoms.*
neutron	*Another small particle found inside atoms.*
electron	*A particle found in an atom that is very much smaller than both protons and neutrons.*
nucleus	*The central portion of an atom that consists of only the protons and neutrons.*
electron cloud	*The space occupied by the electrons surrounding the nucleus.*
element	*Another name for any of the distinct atoms in the periodic table.*
atomic weight	*The total weight of an atom; the weight of the protons and neutrons combined.*

NOTES:

Chapter 2: Molecules

Time Required:

   Text reading - 1 hour
   Experimental - 1 hour

Experimental setup:

   NONE

Additional Materials:

   Small marshmallows
   Large marshmallows

Overall Objectives:

In this chapter the students will explore how atoms combine to make molecules. They will discover that in order to make molecules the atoms must obey certain rules. These rules control how the atoms combine.

2.1 From atoms to molecules

Atoms combine with other atoms to make molecules. The connection between two atoms is called a bond. The specifics of bonding are quite complicated and beyond the scope of this level, so many of the more complicated details will not be discussed. However, some of the general concepts will be introduced.

2.2 Forming bonds

Bonds are formed via the electrons in an atom. When two atoms combine, the spaces surrounding each central core (the electron orbitals) merge. The electrons of each atom share this combined space. The electrons themselves are not always evenly distributed within this space (see Section 2.5), but the space that each electron occupied on a single atom is now combined with the space of the other atom.

The ability of an atom to form a bond with another atom depends on whether or not its electron cloud has enough "space" to accommodate new electrons. For example, the electron orbital of a hydrogen atom can accommodate a total of two electrons. Because a single hydrogen atom has only one electron, it can bond with another hydrogen atom that has one electron to make a molecule such that their combined electron cloud has two electrons. The electron orbitals for both of the hydrogen

atoms become full, and a hydrogen molecule cannot bond with any other atom. Compare this to a helium atom. Helium is a noble gas and cannot bond with any other atom. Why? Because it already has two electrons in its orbital and there is no space available to accommodate additional electrons. All of the noble gases have "full" orbitals. This is the reason they don't easily bond to other atoms.

2.3 Types of bonds

The two general types of bonds that atoms make are as follows:

1. Shared electron bonds, or covalent bonds

2. Unshared electron bonds, or ionic bonds.

The terms "shared" and "unshared" are descriptive terms used to describe the two general types of bonds: covalent and ionic. Covalent bonds are those bonds made by atoms that mostly share their electrons. Ionic bonds form when one atom "gives up" an electron to another atom and the electrons are essentially unshared.

2.4 Shared electron bonds

Atoms that are identical always make covalent bonds. For example the bond between two hydrogen atoms is covalent, the bond between two carbon atoms is covalent, and the bond between two oxygen atoms is covalent. These atoms form covalent bonds because both of the atoms, being identical, will have the same ability to give away or to receive electrons. Covalent bonds between two identical atoms are "pure" covalent bonds, which means there is equal sharing.

Covalent bonds can also be formed between two atoms that are not alike but that have a similar ability to pull away or give electrons. Oxygen and carbon, for example, form covalent bonds. These bonds are not "pure" covalent bonds. In fact, their electrons are not entirely equally shared since oxygen has a slightly higher tendency to keep more electrons for itself. However, they are still considered to form a covalent bond because the electrons are mostly shared.

2.5 Unshared electron bonds

When atoms do not share electrons, they form ionic bonds. In this case the electrons are almost exclusively on one or the other atom and are not equally shared, or even slightly shared. When an atom has more or fewer electrons than it would normally have, it is called an ion. In a molecule with unequally shared electrons, one atom will have more electrons than it should, and the other atom will have fewer electrons. Each atom is called an ion. The bond is called an ionic bond.

When sodium and chlorine combine, they form an ionic bond, because the electrons are not shared equally. The chlorine wants all of the electrons for itself, and the sodium is willing to give up its electron and just hang out next to the chlorine.

2.6 Bonding rules

The number of bonds and the type of bonds an atom will form depend on the number of electrons available and the type of atoms forming the bonds.

The maximum number of bonds an element can form depends on the number of available electrons. *Available* is emphasized because although an element may have 53 electrons, it cannot form 53 bonds. To form a bond, it takes two electrons, one from each atom. The electron that forms a bond must be available and cannot be part of a full orbital. For example, the element iodine has 53 electrons, but it has only one free electron. The other 52 are not available because they are in filled shells.

At this point, understanding how many electrons make how many bond and which kind is not important, the main point is the following:

Atoms follow rules to form bonds with other atoms.

Here are a few atoms with the number of bonds they typically form:

Hydrogen : 1
Sodium: 1
Beryllium: 2
Boron: 3
Carbon: 4
Nitrogen: 3
Oxygen: 2
Fluorine: 1

Also, though this is not mentioned in the text, some atoms can form double or triple bond. For example, carbon dioxide, CO_2, has two double bonds between carbon and oxygen: O=C=O. Carbon still has 4 bonds and oxygen still has two bonds, but carbon is not bonded to 4 different atoms.

2.7 Shapes of molecules

The molecules that result when two or more atoms combine also have particular shapes. The shapes depend on the number of electrons for each atom and the type of bond they form. Again, the details of how molecules are shaped are not important. The point is,

The shapes of molecules also obey rules.

Some common shapes include:

Carbon with four single bonds: tetrahedral

Carbon with two double bonds: linear

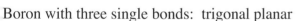

Boron with three single bonds: trigonal planar

Nitrogen with three single bonds: pyramidal

side view   top view

2.8 Summary

Discuss with the students the following main points of this chapter:

- Atoms combine with other atoms to make molecules.

- The connections between atoms in a molecule are called bonds. There are two types of bonds: covalent and ionic.

- Atoms follow rules when they form bonds. The number of bonds an atom can form depends on the number of available electrons on the atom.

- The shapes of molecules also follow rules, and molecules have certain shapes.

Experiment 2:   Making marshmallow molecules   Date:

Objective:

   To learn how atoms fit together by making marshmallow molecules.

Materials:

   small colored marshmallows
   large marshmallows
   toothpicks

Experiment:

1. Take several marshmallows of both sizes and several toothpicks.

2. Make shapes from the marshmallows and toothpicks. First, form any number
   of links between marshmallows - i.e. put any number of toothpicks into each
   marshmallow. Draw the shapes below, noting the number of toothpicks in each
   marshmallow.

Not following any rules.

In this experiment the students will use marshmallows to explore how atoms fit together to make molecules.

Have the students record the date on the top line.

Discuss the objective.

Materials:

   The materials for this experiment are marshmallows and toothpicks.

   Two sizes of marshmallows are preferred, but one size will work.

   Gum drops or jellybeans can also be used.

Experiment:

First, have the students make marshmallow molecules without any rules. Encourage the students to make molecules of various sizes and shapes. They do not need to record every shape they make, but try to get them to draw as many different shapes as they can.

Some suggested shapes are shown on the left.

There are no "wrong" answers as all shapes are valid in this step.

3. Now assign an "atom" to each of the marshmallows. The large marshmallows should be C, N, and O and the small marshmallows should be H and Cl. Use the following "rules" for the number of toothpicks that can go into a marshmallow.

Carbon - 4 toothpicks all pointing away from each other

Nitrogen - 3 toothpicks pointing downward

Oxygen - 2 toothpicks pointing downward

Hydrogen and Chlorine - 1 toothpick pointing in any direction.

Cl or H

4. Next, try to make the following molecules from your marshmallow atoms:

H_2O : This is one oxygen and two hydrogens.
      Follow the rules above, and draw the shape on the following chart:.

NH_3: This is one nitrogen and three hydrogens.
      Follow the rules above, and draw the shape on the following chart:.

CH_4: This is one carbon and four hydrogens
      Follow the rules above, and draw the shape on the following chart:.

CH_3OH: This is one carbon with three hydrogens and one oxygen attached. The oxygen has one hydrogen.
      Follow the rules above, and draw the shape on the following chart:.

Next, the students will make "real" molecule models following specific rules.

The rules for carbon, nitrogen, oxygen, hydrogen and chlorine are shown. Note that the orientation of the bonds (toothpicks) are also important. The students can first try to put the toothpicks into several marshmallows following these rules before making molecules.
Note that the large marshmallows are assigned to carbon, nitrogen and oxygen. If this is confusing, try to differentiate between the molecules by adding a drop of food coloring to each.

Next, the students will make "molecules" with the marshmallow "atoms." Some molecules are given as examples.

The names of these molecules are as follows:

H_2O : water

NH_3: ammonia

CH_4: methane

CH_3OH: methanol

CCl_4: four chlorine atoms with one central carbon (carbon tetra-chloride)

CH_3CH_3: two carbon atoms connected with three hydrogens each
              (ethane)

CH_2Cl_2: two hydrogen atoms and two chlorine atoms all connected to one central carbon atom (dichloromethane).

The correct shapes for the example molecules are displayed on the left.

Have the students note the number of bonds for each molecule and ask them whether or not they followed the rules.

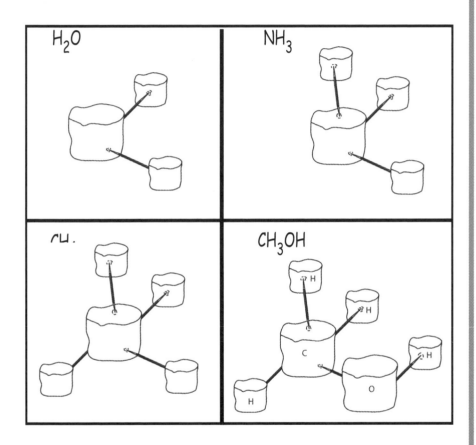

5. Now following the "rules" outlined in step 3 for the marshmallow molecules, make other "molecules." Make as many different shapes as you can without breaking the "rules." Draw your shapes in the boxes below.

CCl_4	CH_3CH_3	
CH_3CH_2OH		

Next, the students will follow the rules and make their own "molecules." Have them note how many bonds each "atom" forms.

Some suggested molecules are the following:

CCl_4 : four chlorine atoms with one central carbon (carbon tetrachloride)

CH_3CH_3: two carbon atoms connected with three hydrogens each (ethane)

CH_3CH_2OH : two carbon atoms with two toothpicks between them, each with two hydrogens. This also obeys the rules (ethanol).

The students can build many different molecules.

Conclusions:

Many different shapes can be made without following the rules.

The large marshmallows can hold up to twenty toothpicks with no rules.

I could only find five shapes (following the rules).

Have the students write some conclusions about the molecules they have created with their marshmallows.

Sample conlusions are given, but these are only examples and not necessarily the conclusions they will find. Help them try to be specific with the conclusions they write.

Emphasize the fact that there should be fewer molecules possible when the atoms obey the rules. "Fewer possible molecules" means that there is not a random arrangement of molecules that make up the world. Atoms have special properties that result in molecules with special properties. Molecules with special properties mean that higher structures, such as tissues, plants, stars, jellyfish, and pudding, also have special properties.

Review

Define the following terms:

molecule   *When two or more atoms are combined.*

bond   *The connection between two atoms.*

ionic bond   *A bond with unshared electrons*

covalent bond   *A bond with shared electrons.*

sodium chloride   *A molecule made by combining sodium and chlorine*
                                  (also known as table salt).

Answer the following questions:

How many bonds does hydrogen typically form?   *One*

How many bonds does carbon typically form?   *Four*

How many bonds does nitrogen typically form?   *Three*

How many bonds does oxygen typically form?   *Two*

Draw the shape of water:

NOTES:

Chapter 3: Chemical Reactions

Time Required:

> Text reading - 1 hour
> Experimental - 1 hour

Experimental setup:

> NONE

Additional Materials:

> Lemon juice
> Balsamic vinegar
> Egg whites
> Baking soda
> Milk
> Sugar
> Salt

Overall Objectives:

In this chapter the students will begin to learn how atoms and molecules react to form and break chemical bonds. It is not important for the students to memorize the names of the reactions. Help them understand that in chemical reactions, the atoms are rearranged. The protons and neutrons are not being changed.

3.1 Introduction

Point out to the students that chemical reactions occur everywhere.

For example:

Stomach acid digests our food.

When hair is straightened or permed, sulfur bonds are broken and reformed.

Cars are powered by the combustion (chemical reaction) of gasoline with oxygen in the air.

When iron is left outside, it reacts with oxygen and rust forms.

Four main divisions of chemical reactions are given. These are called *combination reactions, decomposition reactions, displacement reactions,* and *exchange reactions.* Most chemical reactions fall into these categories or are combinations of these categories.

3.2 Combination reaction

In a combination reaction, two or more molecules combine to form a single product. The example shown is the formation of sodium chloride by combining sodium metal and chlorine gas.

NOTE:
In the reaction between sodium metal and chlorine gas, the chlorine gas is a dimer (two atoms of chlorine). The bond between the chlorine atoms is broken before the formation of sodium chloride, so there is an extra step that is not shown.

3.3 Decomposition reaction

In a decomposition reaction, molecules decompose or "break down" to form other molecules.

Note that two molecules of water decompose into one molecule of oxygen gas and two molecules of hydrogen gas. This is called a balanced reaction because the number of H and O atoms is the same on both sides; only the nature of the bond changes.

3.4 Displacement reaction

A displacement reaction is slightly harder to visualize than the other two reactions because bonds are breaking and reforming at once. In the reaction of water with sodium metal, the sodium atoms displace a hydrogen atom on each of the water molecules. The two free hydrogens then combine to make hydrogen gas (H_2).

Again note that the reaction is balanced in that two water molecules are shown reacting with two sodium atoms giving two molecules of sodium hydroxide and one molecule of hydrogen gas.

3.5 Exchange reaction

In an exchange reaction, the atoms trade places. The example shown is the reaction of hydrochloric acid (HCl) and sodium hydroxide (NaOH). Again, bonds are both breaking and forming in this reaction.

This particular exchange reaction is also an acid-base reaction and will be covered in more detail in subsequent chapters. Hydrochloric acid is a very strong acid and very harmful if swallowed. Sodium hydroxide is a very strong base and also very harmful if swallowed. Both of these will also cause burns on skin. However, when they are added together and react, they make table salt (which we eat) and water. If concentrated reagents are used, the reaction is quite violent and will produce a large amount of heat.

3.6 Spontaneous or not?

Not all reactions occur spontaneously. Some reactions, like the decomposition of water, require energy input before the reaction will proceed. The reasons why one reaction is spontaneous and another is not are beyond the scope of this level. The key concepts are "enthalpy" and "entropy." These are described in a branch of chemistry called chemical thermodynamics.

3.7 Evidences for chemical reactions

There are several indicators that tell scientists when a chemical reaction has taken place. These include bubbles, color change, heat exchange, and precipitation. Sometimes more than one of these can occur at the same time. Both bubbles and heat can be given off together. Sometimes none of them occur and more subtle methods must be used to detect the reaction.

Bubbles form when one of the molecules produced is a gas.

Color changes may indicate a variety of end products. Compounds that contain metals, like copper (Cu), often display color. Blood, for example, contains iron (Fe). When blood is combined with oxygen it is bright red; however, without oxygen it is a darker red.

A solution can either give off heat (exothermic) or take in heat (endothermic). Most exothermic reactions are spontaneous.

Precipitations occur when one or more products of the reaction are no longer soluble in the solution.

3.8 Summary

Discuss with the students the following main points of this chapter:

• Molecules and atoms react with each other to form new molecules.

• There are four basic types of chemical reactions, and these can combine for more complicated reactions.

• Not all reactions occur spontaneously.

• Some chemical reactions can be observed.

Experiment 3:   Identifying Chemical Reactions   Date: _____

Objective:

In this experiment we will try to identify a chemical reaction by observing the changes that occur when two solutions are added together.

Hypothesis:

A chemical reaction can be identified by observing changes that occur in the course of the reaction.

Materials:
baking soda
lemon juice
balsamic vinegar
sugar (1-2 Tbs dissolved in 1/2 cup of water)
salt (1-2 Tbs dissolved in 1/2 cup of water)
egg whites
milk
several small jars
eye dropper

Experiment:

1. Look at the chart in the Results section. Write down all of the items (i.e. baking soda, lemon juice, balsamic vinegar, sugar, salt, and egg whites) horizontally above the boxes of each column.

2. Now write the same list of items vertically down the left side of the grid, next to the boxes for each row.

3. There should be an item assigned to each column and to each row.

4. In the boxes in the middle, record what you observe when the item listed in the column is mixed with the item in the corresponding row.

In this experiment the students will examine chemical reactions and try to identify when they happen.

Select a variety of food items. Bleach and ammonia cause good chemical reactions, but they can give off strong odors and this combination is not recommended.

Have the students put a small amount of each item into a jar.

Have the students examine the contents of each jar.

Note the color and odor wherever possible.

Although most of the items are food items, do not allow the students to taste them.

Have the students record the color, texture, and odor next to each item in the materials list wherever possible.

For example:

Baking Soda: white powder, no odor
Balsamic Vinegar: dark liquid, sour odor

5. Look especially for changes that indicate a chemical reaction has taken place. For example, look for bubbles, color change, or a precipitate.

6. Ask your teacher for the unknown solutions. When you mix them try to determine whether a chemical reaction has taken place. Try to identify what the unknown solutions are.

Results:

	milk	lemon juice	salt water	baking soda	vinegar	egg whites
milk		REACT precipitate	NO	NO	REACT precipitate	NO
lemon juice	REACT precipitate		NO	REACT bubbles	NO	REACT precipitate
salt water	NO	NO		NO	NO	NO
baking soda	NO	REACT bubbles	NO		REACT bubbles	NO
vinegar	REACT precipitate	NO	NO	REACT bubbles		REACT precipitate
egg whites	NO	REACT precipitate	NO	NO	REACT precipitate	

Have the students write the "reagents" on the top and side of the grid. The bottom boxes can be marked out, or each reaction can be performed twice. It might be nice to check the order of addition; add lemon juice to baking soda, then add baking soda to lemon juice, to see if a difference can be observed (the order of addition should not matter). This is optional.

Have the students record their observations in the boxes for each reaction.

JUST FOR FUN:

Watch baking soda decompose and give off carbon dioxide gas while making peanut brittle.

Peanut Brittle

1 1/2 cups sugar
1 cup syrup (white Karo)
1/2 cup water

1 1/2 cups raw peanuts
1 teaspoon soda
buttered pan

Boil sugar, water and syrup in a sauce pan on medium heat until it turns a little brown. Add 1 1/2 cups raw peanuts. Stir until golden brown. Don't over brown. Add 1 teaspoon soda. Spread in buttered pan.

Unknowns:

Descriptions

._____

2._____

Result when the two are mixed:_____

What could they be?_____

Conclusions:

_____

_____

_____

_____

_____

_____

Give the students two "unknowns." These can either be two that will react or two that won't react. It can be done more than once. The students may want to give you an "unknown" to see if you can identify it.

Explain to the students that much of the time scientists are trying to figure out how to identify unknowns. The students have observed all of the reactants both before and after a reaction. They now have the necessary knowledge to identify an unknown.

Another option is to give the students only one unknown. Have them guess what it might be before performing any tests. Then have the student test this unknown with each of the other reactants. Have them prove the identity of the unknown with the chemical reactions they have already observed.

Have the students write valid conclusions. Help them state conclusions that reflect only the data found in this experiment. For example, "Salt water does not react with anything" is not a valid conclusion because we haven't tested everything. However, "Salt water does not react with any of the items we tested" is valid.

Review

What are the four types of chemical reactions?

decomposition reaction
combination reaction
displacement reaction
exchange reaction

Define the following terms:

chemical reaction   *A process where chemical bonds are broken or created between atoms and molecules.*

combination reaction   *A reaction in which two molecules combine to form a single product.*

decomposition reaction   *A reaction in which a molecule breaks apart to make two or more new molecules.*

displacement reaction   *A reaction in which one atom releases another atom from a molecule.*

exchange reaction   *A reaction in which one atom trades places with another atom on a different molecule.*

spontaneous   *Term describing when a reaction happens automatically.*

List four changes that can be observed when a chemical reaction has taken place.

bubbles forming
color change
temperature change
precipitate formation

Chapter 4: Acids, Bases, and pH

Time Required:

    Text reading - 30 minutes
    Experimental - 1 hour
    Experimental setup: 0.5 hours

Experimental setup:

    cooking pot for boiling water

Additional Materials:

    One head of red cabbage
    Distilled water
    The following solutions:
        Ammonia
        Mineral water
        Vinegar
        Soda pop
        Milk

Overall Objectives:

This chapter introduces acids, bases, pH and pH indicators. It is not important that the students understand the details of an acid-base reaction. This chapter will serve as an introduction to the overall concepts and terminology.

4.1 Introduction

An acid-base reaction is a type of exchange reaction. In the example on page 21, the hydrogen atom from acetic acid trades places with the sodium atom from sodium bicarbonate. Explain to the student that vinegar is a type of acid, called acetic acid, and baking soda is a type of base. The formal name for baking soda is *sodium bicarbonate.*

Discuss with the students which atoms change places. Show them from the drawing that hydrogen exchanges places with sodium. Explain that the other atoms remain the same.

NOTE:

The molecules are not drawn with the bonds showing, and on first inspection it appears that the central carbon on both molecules has broken the rule of "4 bonds for carbon." Also, two of the oxygens appear to have broken the rule for "2 bonds for oxygen." However, in each case the bond between the central carbon atom and one of the oxygen atoms is a double bond. Double bonds are beyond the scope of the this level, but all of the bonding rules are satisfied.

4.2 The pH scale

The pH scale is important, but mathematically and conceptually the actual definition of pH is too difficult for this level. pH is pronounced by just saying the letters "P" and "H." pH is actually a measure of the hydrogen ion concentration (written as [H]). The mathematical expression for pH is:

$$pH = -\log [H]$$

The higher the hydrogen ion concentration, the lower the pH, the lower the hydrogen ion concentration, the higher the pH. The hydrogen ion concentration is the real definition of what is meant by "acid" in this chapter.

The chart on page 22 of the student text shows the pH for various solutions. Discuss the chart with the students. Show them that many of the foods we eat are near neutral pH. Show them that some foods are acidic, like vinegar. Explain to the students that this is why vinegar has a very strong sour taste.

Discuss with the students some other items and their pH. For example, explain that both oranges and lemons are acidic, but the medicine used to treat an upset stomach is basic.

Other items not on the chart:

Lemons - pH 2.4

Oranges - pH 3.4

Seawater - pH 8.5 to 10

Milk of magnesia - pH 10.5

4.3 Properties of acids and bases

The properties of acids and bases are quite different, and in many ways opposite.

Acids are sour, not slippery, and effective in dissolving metals.

Bases are bitter, slippery, and reactive with metals to form precipitates.

Students should NOT taste solutions to determine if they are acids or bases. Before modern techniques were available, many chemists tasted things to find out more about them. However, this is quite dangerous, and today scientists do not taste anything in the laboratory.

If the students want to test the slipperiness of a solution, a household cleaner like ammonia can be diluted 1:10 and they can feel the difference between this and vinegar. Proton concentration (or pH) is the real definition of what we mean by "acid" in this chapter.

4.4 Measuring pH

Scientists measure pH with pH meters, pH paper, or solution indicators.

The most common laboratory technique for measuring pH is to use a pH meter. There are a variety of pH meters and electrodes available. The most common electrode is called a glass electrode. There is a small glass ball at the end of this electrode that senses the pH electrically.

Before pH meters, pH paper was the most common way to measure pH. Litmus paper can still be found in most laboratories together with other types of pH paper. There are two types of litmus paper. The blue litmus tests for acidic solutions and the red tests for basic solutions. Litmus paper is not suitable for determining the exact pH; it can only indicate if a solution is acidic or basic. Other types of pH paper can more accurately determine the actual pH.

Litmus paper is made with a compound called an indicator. An indicator is any molecule that changes colors as a result of a pH change.

The table gives some common indicators used in the laboratory. Some of these are difficult to pronounce, but many can be looked up in a dictionary or encyclopedia for pronunciation guidance.

The chart on page 24 of the student text is meant to illustrate that there are a variety of pH indicators that can be used over a wide range of pH. Often pH indicators are mixed so that more than one pH range can be detected.

4.5 Summary

Discuss the following main points of this chapter with the students:

- An acid-base reaction is a special kind of exchange reaction. Have the students look again at the illustration in section 4.1 and discuss how the atoms on each molecule trade places.

- pH measures the acidity or basicity of a solution. Have the students look again at the pH of a base, the pH of an acid, and the pH of a neutral solution.

- Review the various methods for measuring pH; pH paper, pH meters, and pH indicators.

NOTES:

Experiment 4:   Making an acid-base indicator   Date: _____

Objective: _We will make an acid-base indicator from red cabbage and use it to determine which solutions are acidic or basic._

Hypothesis: _We can use an indicator to identify acidic or basic solutions._

Materials:
- half a head of red cabbage
- distilled water
- small jars
- coffee filters
- eye dropper
- various solutions: for example,
  - ammonia
  - mineral water
  - vinegar
  - soda pop
  - milk

Experiment:

1. Take half of the head of red cabbage and divide it into several pieces.

2. Place three cups of distilled water in a pan, and bring the water to a boil.

3. Place the cabbage in the boiling water and boil for several minutes.

4. Remove the cabbage and let the water cool. The water should be a deep purple color.

5. Take one cup of the cabbage water for this experiment and REFRIGERATE the rest for the next experiment.

6. Cut the coffee filters into small strips, about 2 cm wide and 4 cm long. Make at least 20.

Have the students write their own objective and hypothesis for this experiment. Some examples are given.

The following list of items is recommended:

    ammonia
    mineral water
    vinegar
    soda pop
    milk

These are both acids and bases and milk is neutral.

Other suggested items include:

    water (neutral)
    Windex or other glass cleaner (basic)
    Lemon juice, or orange juice (acidic)
    White grape juice (acidic)

The cabbage water produces enough material for this experiment and the one in Chapter 5. It is important to refrigerate the cabbage juice, or it will spoil and cannot be used for the next experiment. It should keep about two weeks in the refrigerator.

Make 20 or more paper strips in case more solutions will be tested. The cabbage indicator can be added to the strips of paper several times and dried in between. This makes the color change more dramatic.

7. With the eye dropper, put several drops of the cabbage mixture onto the filter papers and allow them to dry. They should be slightly pink and uniform in color. If the papers are too light, more solution can be dropped onto them and then they can be dried again. This is your acid indicator paper.

8. Label one of the jars "Control Acid" and place a tablespoon of vinegar into the jar. Add 5 tablespoons of water. This is your *known* acid.

9. Label another jar "Control Base" and add a tablespoon of ammonia to the jar. Add 5 tablespoons of water. This is your *known* base.

10. Put one tablespoon of the other solutions you have collected into separate jars and add 2 to 5 tablespoons of water to each.

11. Carefully dip the pH paper into the "Control Acid" and record your results. Look immediately at the paper for a color change. Tape the paper in the book under "Control Acid."

12. Carefully dip a new piece of pH paper into the "Control Base" and record your results. Look immediately for a color change. Tape the paper in the book under "Control Base."

13. Now take new pH paper and dip it into the other solutions you have made. Record your results. Tape the papers into the book.

Results:

Item	color of pH paper	Acid/Base?	Notes
Control Acid	*pink*	*acid*	
Control Base	*green*	*base*	

In this experiment the students are introduced to "controls." A control is an experiment where the outcome is already known, or where a given outcome can be determined. The control provides a point of reference or comparison for the experiments using unknowns. For example, in this experiment the students will test for acidity or basicity with a pH indicator, but they do not know what the expected color change will be. By doing controls, with solutions that they know are either acidic (vinegar) or basic (ammonia), they can determine what the color change for an acid is and what the color change for a base is. Only then can the test for the "unknown" solutions.

Control experiments also tell the scientist when the experiment has failed. If no color change is observed with a control, something is wrong with the setup or design of the experiment. Control experiments help scientists check for errors.

The ammonia (control base) should turn the paper green.
The vinegar (control acid) should turn the paper pink.

The color change observed on the pH paper may be quick or it may be subtle. It is best to look at the paper immediately after it has been dipped into the solution. If it is too difficult to determine what the color change on the paper is, the cabbage indicator can be used directly. Simply pour a small amount (a teaspoon or two) into the solution directly and record the color change.

Item	color of pH paper	Acid/Base?	Notes

Help the students be specific and make valid conclusions from their data. If something did not change color, but the experimental controls worked, it is probably true that the solution is neutral or near neutral. However, if no color change is observed or if the result is ambiguous, it may not be true that the solution is neutral, or it may be that it is just difficult to tell.

Have the students draw conclusions even if they experienced difficulties.

Conclusions: *(The following are examples of valid conclusions.)*

Ammonia is basic. Basic solutions turn green with the cabbage indicator.

Vinegar is acidic. Acidic solutions turn pink with the cabbage indicator.

Grape juice turned the paper purple. Because grape juice is already purple, it cannot be concluded from this experiment if grape juice is acidic, basic, or neutral.

Review

Define the following terms:

electrode   *The part of the pH meter that goes directly into the solution that detects the pH of the solution.*

pH meter   *An instrument that measures pH.*

litmus paper   *A special paper that can be used to measure pH.*

acid-base indicator *Any solution that changes color as a result of pH.*

acid-base reaction   *A special type of exchange reaction between and acid and a base.*

control   *A reaction, or test ,whose outcome is already known.*

Answer the following questions:

What is the pH of a neutral solution?   *seven*

What is the pH of an acidic solution?   *less than seven*

What is the pH of a basic solution?   *more than seven*

Is vinegar an acid or a base?   *Vinegar is an acid.*

Is baking soda an acid or a base?   *A solution of baking soda is basic.*

What is the chemical name for vinegar? *acetic acid*

What is the chemical name for baking soda? *sodium bicarbonate*

NOTES:

Chapter 5: Acid-Base Neutralization

Time Required:

    Text reading - 1 hour
    Experimental - 30 minutes

Experimental setup:

    Acid-base indicator made in
    Experiment 4

Additional Materials:

    Ammonia
    Vinegar

Overall Objectives:

In this chapter the students will be introduced to additional details about the acid-base reaction of vinegar and baking soda. The students will also be given a chance to plot data and perform an acid-base titration in the experimental section of this chapter.

5.1 Introduction

On page 26 of the student text the overall reaction for acetic acid (vinegar) and sodium bicarbonate (baking soda) is shown. Have the students look carefully at the drawing and note the various steps.

The main points to emphasize on this page are as follows:

- Acids and bases neutralize each other to make "salt" and water.

- This particular acid-base reaction (vinegar and baking soda) is actually TWO reactions; an exchange reaction and a decomposition reaction. (See Chapter 3.)

- The pH of the final solution is 7 (neutral) if equal concentrations and amounts of acid and base are combined.

The decomposition portion of the reaction is marked in the gray dotted box. The bubbles that are released from the reaction are carbon dioxide, (CO_2), and the solution that remains is water and sodium acetate, a salt. Sodium acetate is NOT the same as table salt.

5.2 Concentration

Here the students will be introduced to concentration.

The concentration of something is simply the number of molecules in a given volume. A bottle of concentrated hand soap, for example, has more soap molecules (or less water) in it than one that is not concentrated. Because it is more concentrated, it takes less soap to make a lather than a less concentrated product; but it is still the same soap.

The same is true for acids and bases. If a solution is concentrated, it has more molecules in it that make it either acidic or basic. Therefore it is stronger.

This is illustrated with the difference between glacial acetic acid (concentrated acetic acid) and vinegar (dilute acetic acid). Glacial acetic acid has a very pungent odor and will burn skin on contact. Vinegar is the same acid, but much less concentrated and safe to eat.

The neutralization process of acids and bases are used in everyday life. Antacids are bases that are used to neutralized the hydrochloric acid in the stomach.

5.3 Titration

On page 28 of the student text the students are introduced to titrations. A titration is a technique where one substance is added to another substance in small quantities. By adding the second substance in small quantities, any small change in the solution conditions, or other properties, can be observed. The technique of titration is used not only for acid-base reactions and other reactions as well.

For an acid-base reaction, the concentration of an unknown acid or base can be determined by doing a titration. How does this work? Acids and bases neutralize each other. If you start with an acid solution and add a base, the base will neutralized the acid. Once all of the acid has been neutralized the next drop of base will cause teh pH to change dramatically. If the concentration of one solution (acid or base) is known, then the concentration of the other unknown solution can be determined.

It is not important that the students fully grasp this concept. It is enough for them to know that an acid and a base will neutralize each other. An example of plotting data is given since plotting will be used in the experimental section of this chapter.

5.4 Plotting data

Organizing data into plots, charts, and diagrams is very important for understanding data. It is a basic scientific skill, and students should be able to organize and plot data.

There are many different ways to plot data. The example given on page 9 of the student text is a simple line plot. A bar graph could also work for this illustration. Another type of plot is a pie chart.   All of these are used to illustrate data in a way that makes it easier to understand.

In this example the height and age of several people are collected. The data are shown in the small table above the plot. Show the students that it is difficult to tell the connection between age and height just by *looking* at the data in the table. Also, point out that if more data were collected, say over 100 people, it would be very difficult to tell what the data show.

Next discuss the plot at the bottom of the page. Tell the students that the plot is a way to visualize the data to make it easier to understand. The two axes are height and age. Show them that for every person a height and age are given and that these two data values intersect at a point on the plot. In this way all of the data from the table can be transferred to the plot.

Discuss how a line can be drawn to connect the points on the plot and this line helps show that as age goes up, height goes up only to a point and does not continue like age, but instead height levels off.

5.5 Plot of an acid-base titration

On page 30 of the student text is a typical plot of an acid-base titration. In this plot the base is added to a fixed volume of acid. Note that the pH stays mostly the same until enough base has been added to neutralize the acid. In this plot, the acid is neutralized after about 10 teaspoons of base has been added. This endpoint will vary depending on the concentration of acid in the initial solution. If only a little acid is present, the endpoint will occur much sooner; if a lot more acid is present, the endpoint will occur later.

The students will perform a titration in the experiment for this chapter and it will look somewhat like this one. The vertical scale will not be pH, but color change.

How does this help determine the concentration of an unknown base or acid?

Recall that the endpoint is where the base has completely neutralized the acid. If the concentration of the base is known, and from the plot, the volume of base added is also known, then the concentration of acid can be calculated using this simple formula:

(volume of base) x (concentration of base) =
          (volume of acid) x (concentration of acid)

It is not important for the students to grasp this formula at this point. However, they should see the "formula" and know it can be calculated.

5.6 Summary

Discuss with the students the following main points of this chapter:

- In an acid-base reaction, the acid and base are neutralized. This means that neither the acid nor the base remains acidic or basic. The neutralization of acids and bases gives salt and water.

- Complete neutralization occurs only when the amount of acid equals the amount of base. When the amount of acid equals the amount of base, the resulting solution is neutral.

- The concentration of an unknown acid or base can be determined by doing a titration. This simply means that because equal amounts of acid and base neutralize each other, an unknown concentration of base (or acid) can be determined using a known concentration of acid (or base). Experiment 5 illustrates this concept.

Experiment 5 : Vinegar and ammonia in the balance: Date:
An introduction to titrations

Objective: *To determine how much ammonia is needed to change the color of vinegar from red to green with the use of an indicator.*

Hypothesis: *An indicator can be used to observe the acid-base reaction of vinegar and ammonia.*

Materials:
    red cabbage indicator (from Experiment 4)
    household ammonia
    vinegar
    small jars
    measuring spoons

Experiment:

1. Measure out 1/4 cup of vinegar and put it into one of the small jars.

2. Add enough of the red cabbage indicator to get a deep red color.

3. With the measuring spoons, carefully add one teaspoon of the ammonia to the vinegar solution. Swirl gently and record the color of the solution.

4. Add another teaspoon of ammonia to the vinegar and record the color of the solution.

5. Keep adding ammonia to the vinegar and record the color of the solution for every teaspoon you add.

6. When the color has changed from red to green, stop adding ammonia.

7. Plot the data on the graph. The horizontal axis should be labeled "Teaspoons of Ammonia" and the vertical axis should be labeled "Color of Solution."

In this experiment, the students will perform an acid-base titration using a cabbage water indicator.

In this experiment the students will write their own hypothesis. Help them think about the material in this section and write a suitable hypothesis. An example is given.

The red cabbage indicator from Experiment 4 is required. If the indicator is too old (more than several weeks, or has mold or bacteria growing in it), fresh cabbage indicator should be made. (See Chapter 4.)

A large glass jar is recommended for the titration.

An eye dropper can be used instead of measuring spoons if desired but students will need to add droperfuls instead of "drops."

NOTE:

This titration can be tricky if the concentration of the base is too dilute. A quick test can be performed by the teacher without the students' observation. Take the 1/4 cup of vinegar and add indicator to the mixture. See that it turns red. Add the 1/4 cup ammonia directly to the acid-indicator mixture. The color should turn green, but if the color is still red, add another 1/4 cup of ammonia. It should turn green; however, if it does not, dilute the vinegar with 1/2 cup water and repeat the above steps. This quick "titration" will help determine how much total ammonia is needed to neutralize the acid. A 1/4 cup is equal to roughly 12-14 teaspoons. Adjust the titration so that not much more than 1/4 cup is needed. Less is all right, but the students will get frustrated if they have to add more than 20 teaspoons; and the best part of the titration is the last part.

8. For every teaspoon added, mark the graph with a round dot the corresponding color.

9. When all of the data have been plotted, connect the dots.

Have the students record the color of the solution with each teaspoonful of ammonia added. The color stays mostly red, then a little purple, and finally turns all green. The transition is quite striking

Results:

Have the students continue adding ammonia to prove see that the color stays green.

Number of Teaspoons	Color
1	red
2	red
3	red
4	red
5	red
6	red
7	red
8	red
9	red/purple
10	red/purple
11	purple/green
12	green
13	green
14	green
15	green
16	green

Extra page for more data to be collected if necessary.

Graphing your data:

On the graph below record the number of teaspoons (horizontal axis) corresponding to the color of the solution (vertical axis).

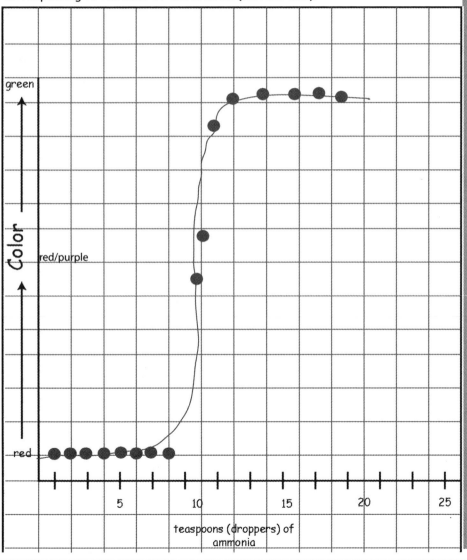

The data should look something like that shown in the plot. Many points lie along the bottom left of the plot, then one or two points will be in the middle. Finally, several will be along the top right-hand edge of the plot.

Have the students connect the points with a smooth curved line. Their plot should look similar to the plot in this section. Point out the following points on the graph:

1. Left-hand lower portion of the plot, the solution is acidic.

2. Middle portion, where the line is going upward, the solution is between acidic and basic (near neutral).

3. Upper right-hand corner, the solution is basic.

Point out that we know this because the color of the indicator is known at various pH values, as we observed in Chapter 4.

Conclusions:

It took 15 teaspoons to turn the solution green.
It took 15 teaspoons to neutralize the vinegar with ammonia.
The amount of ammonia required to neutralize the vinegar was equal to the amount of vinegar used.

Help the students make valid conclusions. Some examples are given. Have the students write down the amount of ammonia it took to neutralize the vinegar. Note whether this equals the amount of vinegar that was used (1/4 cup).   Here are some equivalent amounts:

3 tsp. = 1 T
4 T = 1/4 cup
12 tsp. = 1/4 cup
1 tsp. = 2 droppers full

Depending on the brands of vinegar and ammonia used, the amounts are often equal.

Review

Define the following terms:

neutralization reaction *One type of exchange reaction such as an acid-base reaction.*

concentration *The number of molecules in a given volume.*

concentrated *Many molecules in a given volume.*

dilute *Few molecules in a given volume.*

Glacial acetic acid *Concentrated acetic acid.*

indigestion *Stomach pain caused by excess acid.*

titration *An experimental technique; can be used to determine concentration for acid-base reaction.*

axes (axis) *The vertical and horizontal lines on a plot that tell what is to be plotted.*

NOTES:

Chapter 6: Mixtures

Time Required:

       Text reading - 1 hour
       Experimental - 30 minutes

Experimental setup:

       NONE

Additional Materials:

       Vinegar
       Vegetable oil
       Rubbing alcohol
       Ammonia
       Melted butter

Overall Objectives:

In this chapter the students will learn about different types of mixtures and what makes something mix or not mix.

6.1 Introduction

Most of the things we encounter in daily life are mixtures, rather than pure substances. The example given is cake. From the outside, cake looks like it is one substance, but it is actually a mixture of many different things.

Discuss with the students other things that are mixtures such as other foods, shampoo, most commercial cleaning fluids, and concrete.

JUST FOR FUN

Have the students bake a cake and let them mix the ingredients:

All natural substances like eggs, flour, milk and chocolate are also mixtures of many different kinds of molecules.

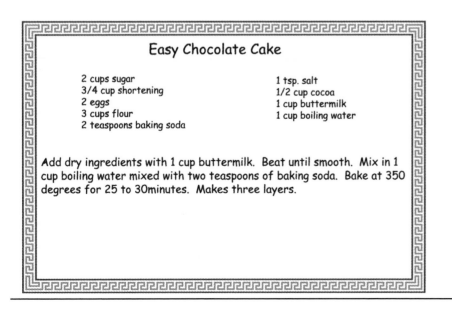

Easy Chocolate Cake

2 cups sugar
3/4 cup shortening
2 eggs
3 cups flour
2 teaspoons baking soda

1 tsp. salt
1/2 cup cocoa
1 cup buttermilk
1 cup boiling water

Add dry ingredients with 1 cup buttermilk. Beat until smooth. Mix in 1 cup boiling water mixed with two teaspoons of baking soda. Bake at 350 degrees for 25 to 30minutes. Makes three layers.

6.2 Types of mixtures

Two types of mixtures are discussed. They are homogeneous mixtures and heterogeneous mixtures. Homogeneous mixtures are mixtures where the molecules are evenly distributed throughout the mixture. Saltwater is an example of a homogeneous mixture. Other examples include the following:

    alchohol-water mixtures
    sugar-water mixtures
    vinegar
    household ammonia

Heterogeneous mixtures are those mixtures where the molecules are not evenly distributed throughout the mixture. Ice water is an example of a heterogeneous mixture. Other examples include:

    sand
    concrete
    ice cream floats
    salad dressing

Another mixture that looks homogeneous but is actually heterogeneous is milk. Milk is a colloid. A colloid has very small molecules suspended in it that are not evenly distributed in solution and are too small to see with our eyes. All colloids are heterogeneous and are cloudy. True homogeneous solutions are clear or colored but not cloudy.

6.3 Like dissolves like

"Like" in this context means that both substances are either polar or charged. (See next page for definition of "polar.")

"Unlike" means that one substance is made of polar, or charged, molecules and the other is made of nonpolar, or uncharged, molecules.

The rule states that substances that are alike will dissolve in one another and substances that are not alike will not dissolve in one another.

A molecule with a positive (+) end and a (-) end is a polar molecule.

Polar simply means having two opposite directions or natures. In the case of molecules, polar means that there are two oppositely charged ends.

Water is very polar. All OH ends are also very polar wherever they occur on a molecule. Molecules with these OH ends will easily mix with water. Methanol (wood alcohol) has the structure CH_3 -OH and mixes easily with water because of the OH at the end.

Other molecules that are also polar in water are acetic acid and sugar. Both of these molecules contain polar OH groups, and both easily dissolve in water.

Most of the vegetable oil molecule is not charged. Point out the long chains (blue) and discuss that these chains are not polar (charged). The C-O bonds (red) in the vegetable oil are slightly polar, but not polar enough to allow the oil to dissolve in water.

Mineral oil is made of only carbons and hydrogens. This molecule has no polar groups at all and will not dissolve in water.

Many cleaning fluids are based on the principle that like dissolves like. Cleaning fluids that are used to clean things other than water-based products are generally nonpolar. Mineral oil cleans oil-based paints because mineral oil is nonpolar.

6.4 Soap

The most common soap or detergent is SDS (sodium dodecyl sulfate or sodium lauryl sufate). Many soaps, shampoos, and detergents contain SDS, and it will be listed as a primary ingredient.

The main point to emphaisize in this section is that soap "allows" oils to dissolve in water. It does this by forming tiny oil droplets that are suspended in the surrounding water. These little oil droplets can then be washed away by the excess water.

6.5 Summary

Discuss with the students the following main points for this chapter:

- There are main two types of mixtures: homogeneous and heterogeneous. Homogeneous mixtures are the same throughout and heterogeneous mixtures are not.

- If two things are "like" each other, they will mix more readily than with things that are not alike.

- Things that are alike will dissolve in each other. Dissolve means to loosen and separate the molecules of one substance so that it can mix into another substance.

- Soap can mix with both oil and water. This allows soap to "dissolve" oil in water.

Experiment 6:   Mix it up!   Date: _____

Objective: *We will observe which solutions mix and which do not.*
               _____

Hypothesis: *Oil will not dissolve in water without soap.*
               Vegetable oil and butter will mix, but oil and water will not mix.

Materials:
    vinegar
    rubbing alcohol
    ammonia
    vegetable oil
    melted butter
    several small jars
    food coloring
    dish soap

Experiment:

Part I: See what mixes.

1. The grid in the Results section is labeled with the following terms along the top and sides of the grid.: water, vinegar, rubbing alcohol, ammonia, vegetable oil, and melted butter,

2. Take out 6 small jars and add 1/4 cup of each item to separate jars. Label the jars.

3. Add a drop of food coloring to each jar.

4. Mix one tablespoon of the uncolored items with 1 tablespoon of each colored item. Record in the boxes whether or not the two items mix.

In this experiment the students will observe different mixtures.

The objective is left blank. To help the students write a suitable objective for this experiment, have them first read the experiment carefully. A suggested objective is listed.

The hypothesis is also left blank. Help the students write a suitable hypothesis. To help them, discuss the main points of this chapter:

- most things are mixtures
- like dissolves like
- soap helps oil dissolve in water

Two suggestions are given.

Materials:

Any of these items can be substituted for other solutions if needed. Try to pick at least two "oily" items and two water-based items.

Results:

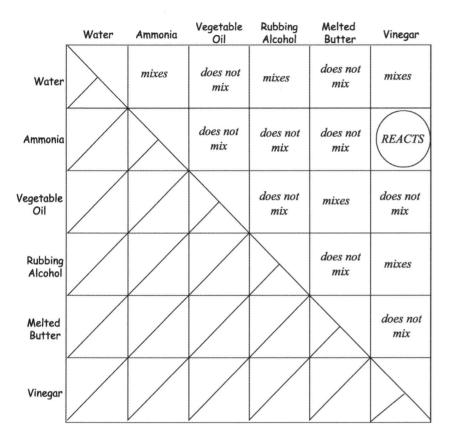

	Water	Ammonia	Vegetable Oil	Rubbing Alcohol	Melted Butter	Vinegar
Water		mixes	does not mix	mixes	does not mix	mixes
Ammonia			does not mix	does not mix	does not mix	REACTS
Vegetable Oil				does not mix	mixes	does not mix
Rubbing Alcohol					does not mix	mixes
Melted Butter						does not mix
Vinegar						

Have the students fill in the grid and note which solutions mix and which do not.

The groups that will mix are as follows:

- water, ammonia, rubbing alcohol, and vinegar

- vegetable oil and melted butter

NOTE:
Ammonia and vingear will react. This is an acid base reaction. They also mix.

Part II: Soap, oil, and water.
1. Put 1/4 cup of water into one of the small glass jars. Add one drop of food coloring.
2. Add 1 tablespoon of vegetable oil to the water.
3. Mix the water and oil. Record your results.
4. Add 1 tablespoon of liquid dish soap to the oil/water mixture.
5. Mix thoroughly. Record your results.
6. Add another tablespoon of liquid dish soap to the mixture, and mix thoroughly.
7. Record your results.

Results:

Oil + water: *The oil and water do not mix.*

Oil + water + 1T soap: *The solution is cloudy. Some oil has disappeared, but most of the oil is still visible.*

Oil + water + 2T soap: *The solution is even more cloudy, and more oil has disappeared.*

In this section the students will experiment with soap to dissolve an oil-water mixture.

As mentioned earlier, soap will make a colloidal mixture of oil and water. This will be visible as the soap turns the oil-water mixture cloudy. There will also be some bubbles, but overall, the mixture should begin to turn cloudy.

As more soap is added, less free oil is visible.

Conclusions:

Oil does not mix with water.

Oil forms a heterogeneous mixture with water.

Alcohol mixes with water. Alcohol is "like" water.

Vegetable oil dissolves in butter. Vegetable oil and butter are "like" each other.

Vegetable oil and butter are both "not like" water.

Help the students make valid conclusions based on the data they have collected.

Some suggestions are given.

Help the students make conclusions using the ideas presented in this chapter. Have the students decide which solutions are "like" each other and which are not. Have them record these as their observations.

Review

Define the following terms:

mixture   *Two or more pure substances mixed together.*

homogeneous   *A mixture of the "same kind," like saltwater.*

heterogeneous   *A mixture of the "other kind," like ice water.*

dissolve   *When two or more substances like to mix.*

What does the phrase "like dissolves like" mean? *Two solutions that are "like" each other will dissolve in each other. Two that are not alike, will not dissolve.*

Name two molecules with charged ends. *water and salt*

Name two molecules without charged ends. *vegetable oil and mineral oil*

How does soap work? *Soap is a molecule with a charged end and an uncharged end. Uncharged molecules will dissolve in the uncharged end of a soap molecule, and charged molecules will dissolve in the charged end. A micelle will form, with the oil on the inside, surrounded by water. The oil can then be washed away.*

Draw a micelle.

NOTES:

Chapter 7: Separating Mixtures

Time Required:

    Text reading - 1 hour
    Experimental - 30 minutes

Experimental setup:

    NONE

Additional Materials:

    Ballpoint pens
    Rubbing alcohol
    Cardboard shoebox

Overall Objectives:

Separating mixtures is very important in chemistry; it is a large part of the discipline of Analytical Chemistry. This chapter will introduce several simple techniques used to separate mixtures. These include filtration, evaporation, and chromatography.

7.1 Introduction

Discuss with the students how they might separate different mixtures.

For example,

How would you separate Legos and rocks? *by hand*

How would you separate sand and rocks? *with a sieve*

How would you separate sand and water? *let the water dry out*

Explain to the students that there are different ways to separate mixtures and that they will learn about three: filtration, evaporation, and chromatography.

7.2 Filtration

Filtration is one way to separate mixtures of different sizes. Some common household filters include sieves, cheesecloth, and coffee filters.

The pore size of the filter determines the sizes of things that can be separated. Large pore sizes like those found in sieves, can separate liquids from larger solids like spaghetti or broccoli. It is even possible

with a sieve to separate flour from rice. In this case the sieve would also need to be shaken to loosen the flour from around the rice.

Some examples of molecular sieves include the pores in cell membranes. Cells have tiny holes that allow small molecules, like salt, to flow freely in and out. Larger molecules (like proteins and DNA) cannot get through these pores and are kept inside the cell.

7.3 Evaporation

Evaporation can be used to separate two substances if only one of them evaporates. Salts and water can be separated this way since water evaporates and salt does not. Alcohol and water cannot be separated using this technique since both alcohol and water evaporate. Baking soda and salt cannot be separated this way since neither baking soda nor salt can evaporate.

To explain evaporation, the next section introduces the three basic states of matter: solids, liquids and gases.

7.4 Solids, liquids, and gases

Matter exists in three states: solid, liquid, and gas. For water, these states differ in how tightly packed the molecules are and in how much energy the molecules have. For solid water, ice, the molecules are packed into a crystalline lattice. The molecules in ice are actually less densely packed than in liquid water. However, the water molecules in ice have less energy (and hence are colder) than those in liquid water.

As energy is added to the ice, the water molecules begin to shake and wiggle. This partially overcomes the weak forces that hold the molcules together in a crystal. The water molecules become able to slide past each other and move around. They lose their crystalline order but still remain densely packed. This is what a liquid looks like on the molecular scale.

As more energy is added, the water molecules completely overcome the forces holding them together, and the free molecules move away from each other as a gas. This is what happens during evaporation. The water molecules spread out so thin they are no longer perceptibly different from the air.

7.5 Chromatography

Chromatography is another way to separate mixtures.

Molecules will often "stick" to a solid; we say they adsorb to the solid. Molecules that adsorb differently (either strongly or weakly) to a solid matrix) of some kind can be separated by chromatography. The matrix can be any porous material from paper to specially designed columns used to adsorb gas molecules. The mixture to be separated (ink colors, large molecules, gases, etc.) is exposed to one end of the matrix and allowed to migrate towards the other end. As the solution (or gas) passes over the paper (or column), molecules will move at different speeds, depending on how strongly they adsorb. The faster moving molecules move ahead of the slower moving molecules, separating them.

7.6 Summary

Discuss with the students the following main points of this chapter:

- There are many ways to separate mixutures. This chapter discusses three: filtration, evaporation, and chromatography.

- Filtration uses filters to separate things of different size. A filter can be anything from a metal sieve to a paper coffee filter. The holes in a filter are called pores. The pore size determines what can be separated. Small pores, like those found in coffee filters, can separate water from coffee. However, a sieve cannot be used to separate coffee from water because the pores are too big.

- Evaporation can be used to separate things that evaporate from things that don't. Water evaporates and salt does not, so evaporation can be used to separate salt from water.

- Paper chromatography can be used to separate the colors in ink. This is demostrated in Experiment 7.

- Discuss with the students the three states of matter: solids, liquids, and gases. Discuss how water can be a solid (ice), a liquid (water), and a gas (water vapor or steam). Other things also exist in different states. Carbon dioxide, for example, is a gas at room temperature. However, dry ice is carbon dioxide in solid form.

Experiment 7:   Black is black?   Date: _____

Objective: *To determine the individual colors in various ink mixtures.*
_____

Hypothesis: *Black ink contains only black ink and no other colors.*
Black ink contains all of the colors.
_____

Materials:
  ball point ink pens of various colors, including black
  rubbing alcohol
  coffee filters (white)
  small jars

Experiment:

1. Pour 1/4 cup of alcohol into several small jars.

2. Take the ink pens and remove the thin plastic tube from the inside.

3. Pull off the top or cut the plastic tube in half.

4. Take the tube and swirl the end of it in the alcohol. Watch that some of the color gets dissolved in the alcohol, but don't let it get too colored.

5. Cut the coffee filter paper into thin strips 1/4 to 1/2 inch wide and 5 to 6 inches long.

6. Place the ends of the strips into the dissolved ink in the jars and allow the alcohol to migrate upwards. It is fine for the strips to touch the sides of the glass jar, but the alcohol won't migrate past this point. It is better if you can suspend the strips in the alcohol without letting the sides touch. To do this tape the strips to the inside of a cardboard box and suspend them in the glass jars.

7. The colors in the ink will migrate up the absorbent strips. Let the strips sit in the alcohol overnight.

In this experiment the students will use paper chromatography to separate the individual colors in inks.

Have the students state an objective. To do this, they need to read through the experiment before beginning. An example is given.

Have the students state a hypothesis. Specifically ask them to predict what colors will be in black ink. Ask them what colors they think black ink contains. Help them write a hypothesis based on their prediction. Some examples are given.

Multicolored ballpoint pens work best. Try to find one with at least 7 or 8 different colors. Don't buy an expensive pen because it will be taken apart for the experiment. If a multicolored pen cannot be found, regular Bic® pens can be used. Black, blue, red and green will give enough colors to compare. Ballpoint pens work better than felt tip pens or markers.

It is important not to let the color of the alcohol-ink mixture get too dark. A quick swirl with the open end of the pen is usually enough.

The ink will not migrate past the point where the paper touches the side of the jar. To avoid holing up the ink's progress place the jars on the inside of a cardboard box with the papers suspended from above the solutions.

Results:

Tape the strips of paper below.
Write the original ink color and record the different colors that each is made of.

Example

Orange
Ink
made of
yellow
and red

After the ink has had a chance to migrate up the paper and once the paper has dried, the students can tape them directly into the book.

Have the students write the original ink color directly on the paper and then write which colors have separated out of the ink.

Have them note which colors make up black. Depending on the brand of pen, the black ink should show all colors or nearly all colors. Brown also shows all colors.

Most of the other colors will be a mixture of fewer colors. Depending on the brand of pen, these colors may also be a mixture of similar colors. For example, a blue pen may show a mixture of only a dark blue and a light blue.

Repeat the previous steps with an unknown sample of ink. Compare your results with those above and try to determine the colors in your unknown ink sample.

Unknown	Color in the unknown:

Now give the students an unknown. Make the unknown without letting the students observe. The unknown can contain inks from two different pens. If a mixture of two colors is to be used, first swirl each in alcohol and then mix the two alcohol solutions.

Suggest that the students give you an unknown. Several unknowns can be set up overnight.

Using the pattern of colors from the known pens, help the students try to identify which pen was used for the unknown.

Conclusions:

_____

_____

_____

_____

_____

_____

_____

_____

Help the students make valid conclusions based on the data they have collected. Help them be specific. For example,

- Black ink from Brand X is made of red, yellow, black, and brown.

- Red ink from Brand X is made of red and pink.

- Blue ink from Brand Y has only blue ink in it.

Ask whether or not they proved or disproved their hypothesis.

Discuss those conclusions that are not valid. For example,

- All black ink has yellow in it. This is not valid based on these data; not all black ink has been tested.

- Blue inks contain only blue. Again, not all blue inks have been tested.

Have the students write any sources of error. For example,

- All of my alcohol went away and no dye went up the paper.

- The papers fell off the box and into the solution.

Review

Define the following terms:

sieve   *A metal bowl with holes in it; a type of filter.*

filter   *Anything that can be used to separate things of different sizes, such as coffee filters, mesh, sieves, or cheesecloth.*

filtration   *A process to separate things of different size.*

pore   *The holes in a filter.*

solid state   *The state of matter ihat exists when the molecules are tightly packed.*

gaseous state   *The state of matter in which the molecules are apart from each other.*

liquid state   *The state between the gaseous state and the solid state; the molecules are more loosely packed than in a solid.*

chromatography   *A technique used to separate different moleclues.*

separation   *The process of taking one or more things out of a mixture.*

NOTES:

Chapter 8: Energy Molecules

Time Required:

Text reading - 1 hour
Experimental - 30 minutes

Experimental setup:

NONE

Additional Materials:

Raw foods such as:
bread
celery
banana
potato

Overall Objectives:

This chapter will introduce "energy" molecules. Energy molecules are those molecules that fuel our bodies, such as carbohydrates and starches.

8.1 Introduction

Some of the words are difficult to pronounce and can be intimidating. Also, these molecules are more complicated than those we have examined previously. It is not important that the students remember all of the names or understand all of the chemical structures. The main points are as follows:

- Carbohydrates are energy molecules.

- Carbohydrates are made mostly of carbon, hydrogen, and oxygen.

- Small carbohydrates are sugars.

- Large carbohydrates are starches and cellulose.

- Starches and cellulose are long chains of smaller carbohydrates (sugars).

8.2 Nutrients

Discuss the various types of foods we eat to get our *nutrients* (i.e., those foods that help our bodies grow and live). Have the students list some of their favorite foods and ask them what kinds of nutrients they think those foods might have. For example,

Carrots have vitamin A.
Milk and meat have protein.
Oranges and lemons have vitamin C.
Eggs have protein.
Milk and sardines have calcium.

8.3 Carbohydrates

Carbohydrates are made of carbon atoms and water molecules. For example, glucose, a simple sugar, has 6 carbons, 6 oxygens, and 12 hydrogens. A chemical formula for glucose can be written as $C_6(H_2O)_6$. This formula shows that glucose has 6 carbon atoms and 6 molecules of water. This is the origin of the name "carbo-hydrate."

The simple carbohydrates are the monocacharides (mon-o-sac´cha-rides).
Larger carbohydrates are the oligosaccharides (o-li-go-sac´cha-rides).

Monosaccharides are very important for our metabolism. They are an essential component in many biochemical pathways. For humans, simple sugars are essential for brain development. Human milk, for example, has the highest sugar content of all animal milk. Whale and seal milk have lower sugar content and higher fat content than human milk, since fat is essential for protecting these animals from the cold ocean waters.

8.4 Starches

The largest carbohydrates are the polysaccharides (pol-y-sac´cha-rides) which include the starches and cellulose.

The two main energy molecules found in plants, that can be used by humans, are amylose (am´-y-lose) and amylopectin (am´y-lo-pec-tin). These are the two main starches found in potatoes, breads, and pasta.

Amylose has several thousand glucose units hooked together into a long chain or polymer.   For simplicity these are shown as straight chains in the picture, but the real amylose chains are twisted around to form an irregular helical coil.

Amylopectin also contains several thousand glucose units, but instead of being a helical coil, it is branched. The structure for glycogen is very similar to that of amylopectin.

In the experiment that the students will perform for this chapter, it is amylose that is detected by iodine. Amylopectin, glycogen, and cellulose cannot be detected by iodine. The helical coil of amylose interacts with the iodine molecules to give a deep purple or black color. The other starches do not form this coil and therefore cannot be detected by iodine.

8.5 Cellulose

Cellulose is the main structural molecule for plants. Because plants need to have rigid cell walls for support (since they don't have bones), the structure for cellulose is very different from that of starches.

The main difference between the bonding for the starches and cellulose is the orientation of the linkage between individual glucose units. For the starches, the term "down" is given for the students. The actual name of this type of bond is "alpha," and it ahs the symbol α. Starches have α bonds between their glucose units.

The term given to the students for the bonds between the glucose units for cellulose is "up." The actual name for this type of bond is "beta," and it has the symbol β.   Starches have β bonds between their glucose units.

This small difference in how the units are hooked to each other makes a huge difference in their overall shape. As mentioned earelier, the starches are either coils or large branched molecules. In contrast, cellulose molcules form large sheets which can stack on one another. The cell walls in plants are made of layers of parallel cellulose sheets. These layers make the cell wall rigid.

Humans cannot use cellulose for energy molecules. We do not have the necessary enzymes required to break the β linkages of cellulose glucose units. Certain animals have bacteria that break the cellulose linkages for them, so they can simply eat grasses and other plants for their diet. Humans get other nutrients from plants but need to eat other foods for energy molecules.

8.6 Summary

Discuss with the students the following main points of this chapter:

- Carbohydrates are molecules found in potatoes, pasta, and breads that give our bodies "energy." These molecules are made of sugar molecules. The sugar molecules are used by our bodies for energy.

- The smaller carbohydrates, called simple carbohydrates, are the sugars, like fructose and glucose. These are single sugars and provide "quick" energy for our bodies since they are easily broken down. The larger carbohydrates, like starch and amylose, are made of many sugar molecules linked together in a long chain. The fact that they are in a long chain means that they are less quickly used by our bodies, and they can serve as stored energy for later use.

- Cellulose is another large carbohydrate molecule found in grass and other plants. It provides plants cells with rigid walls for stability. Humans cannot use grass as a source of energy because we cannot break the linkages between the glucose units in a cellulose molecule. Cows, horses, and other animals can use grass for food energy because they have bacteria in their gut which breaks the bonds for them.

NOTES:

Experiment 8:   Show me the starch   Date:

Objective: _To determine which foods contain starch._

Hypothesis: _Potatoes conatin starch. Celery does not._

Materials:
      tincture of iodine
      variety of foods including:
          pasta
          bread
          celery
          banana
          potato
          other fruits
      laundry starch
      absorbent paper
      eye dropper
      [Iodine is VERY poisonous, do not eat any food items with iodine.]

Experiment:

1. Take several food items and place them on a cookie sheet.

2. Take the liquid starch and, with the eye dropper, put a small amount on a piece of absorbent paper and label it "Control." Let it dry.

3. Add a droplet of iodine to the starch on the control paper. Record the color.

4. Add iodine to each of the food items and record the color.

5. Compare the color on the "control" to the color of each food item.

6. Note those food items that change color and those that do not.

In this experiment the students will determine which foods contain starch (amylose) and which do not.

Have the student write the objective and hypothesis. Have them guess which foods might have starch and which might not, based on the text for this chapter.   Some examples are given.

Only amylose is detected by iodine, so technically students will be observing only those foods that contain amylose. Iodine is very poisonous so warn the students not to eat any foods that have iodine on them.

Select a variety of food items. Include some that contain amylose, like potatoes or bread. Laundry starch is used as a control. Laundry starch is made of corn starch (which contains amylose) and borax, so it can be used as a positive control. Some papers have amylose in them, so you also need to test the paper alone. Use a paper that does not turn black.

Explain the use of a control to the students. Controls test the experimental method to see if it's working. If the control does not work, something is wrong with the experiment and any other results are not valid. If the control works, then it is more likely that the results of the experiment are real and can be used to draw final conclusions. For example, if the iodine solution were bad, old, or just not working, then even the laundry starch would not turn black. But if no control was performed, the results might indicate that nothing has starch in it. These results would be incorrect, and the conclusion that "potatoes have no starch" would be incorrect. Control experiments are a very important part of real scientific investigation. They are essential for determining the validity of individual experiments.

Results:

	Food Item	Color
Control		

Have the students record their results. Those items containing starch should have a deep purple, almost black color. Everything else will stay light brown.

Conclusions:

_____

_____

_____

_____

_____

_____

Help the students write valid conclusions based on the data they have collected. Have them write down if they proved or disproved their hypothesis.

Some example are:

- Raw potatoes turn black with iodine.
- Potatoes contain starch.
- Raw celery does not turn iodine black.
- Celery does not have starch. [starch here meaning amylose]

OPTIONAL:

Test several items before and after cooking them. Ask the students to predict whether or not cooking will affect the outcome of their results.

Cooking breaks the bonds between glucose units and they should see a difference with cooked foods. Cooked foods should not turn purple.

Review

Define the following terms:

nutrients   *Essential molecules we get from the foods we eat.*

carbohydrate   *Molecule made with carbon, oxygen, and hydrogen.*

monosaccharide   *Molecules of a single sugar like glucose.*

oligosaccharide   *Molecules formed by a "few" sugars, like sucrose; table sugar.*

polysaccharide   *"Many" sugars, like starches and cellulose.*

starch   *Long chains of sugar units; found in plants and animals.*

cellulose   *Long chains of sugar units; found mostly in plants.*

amylose   *A common polysaccharide found in plants such as potatoes.*

amylopectin   *A polysaccharide found in plants.*

NOTES:

Chapter 9: Polymers

Time Required:

Text reading - 1 hour
Experimental - 30 minutes

Experimental setup:

NONE

Additional Materials:

NONE

Overall Objectives:

This chapter introduces polymers. A polymer is any molecule that consists of several repeating units. In the last chapter, energy molecules (carbohydrates) were polymers of glucose units.

The main points from this chapter are as follows:

• Polymers are long molecules of repeating units.

• A polymer's shape determines its properties.

• Polymers can be modified to change properties.

9.1 Introduction

Explain to the students that polymers are long chains of repeating units. Review with them the Greek word root for "poly" and "mer" and explain that *polymer* literally means "many parts."

Discuss with the students items that they know are made of plastic. For example,

    toys
    plastic wrap
    parts of cars
    CD players
    video cases

Explain to them that all of these things are made of polymers.

Have the students discuss those things that might be made of polymers.

These include all plastics, things made of wood, foods, and clothing. Even our bodies contain polymers. (See next chapter.)

Explain to them that there are many different kinds of polymers, both natural and synthetic. Polymers can be chains of identical repeating units like cellulose and starch, but they can also have different kinds of repeating units. (See next chapter.)

9.2 Polymer uses

As we saw in the last chapter, the structure of polymers helps determine its physical properties. Recall that cellulose and starch are made of exactly the same molecules but they are put together differently. This gives them very different properties.

Explain to the students that the different properties that polymers can have makes them very useful. Discuss with them some soft and hard polymers they may know. Explain that these differences are due to differences in the polymer structure.

9.3 Structure of polymers

Differences in structure also affect the properties of synthetic polymers. For example, plastics made of linear chains of polyethylene ("linear" refers to those without side branches) are very different from chains made that contain side branches. Linear chains can pack closely, which makes the plastic hard and stiff. Branched molecules, on the other hand cannot pack together tightly, and this makes the plastic soft.

Some other polymers that are commonly used include the following:

- polypropylene — used in the textile industry to make molds

- polyisoprene — synthetic rubbers

- polystyrene — toys

- polyvinyl chloride — foams, films, and fibers.

9.4 Modifying polymers

Polymer properties can also change simply by hooking the individual polymer chains together.

Explain to the students that the vulcanization of rubber is one such process.

When natural rubber is heated in the presence of sulfur, the long linear chains connect with each other via sulfur bonds. This changes the physical properties of natural rubber.

The vulcanization of rubber causes cross-links in the polymer molecules. They are called cross-links because they link two molecules across the chains.

The number of cross-links can be varied by changing the amount of sulfur added, the heat, and the time the process is allowed.

Rubber products, like surgical gloves and kitchen gloves, are made when few cross-links are added to natural rubber. When more cross-links are added, the rubber becomes stiff enough for bicycle tubes and tires.

Also, the nature of the cross-links gives rubber its elasticity. Rubber bands can be stretched, which stretches out the long polymer chains. However, because of the cross-links, the rubber bands snap back to their original shape and size when released.

9.5 Summary

Discuss with the students the following main points of this chapter:

- "Polymer" is a general term describing many different molecules. Polymers include the carbohydrates from Chapter 8, plastics, and proteins and DNA from Chapter 10.

- Polymers can be put together in different ways. They can be long, linear chains, they can have side branches, or they can be connected to each other. These different shapes give polymers different properties.

- Polymer properties can be modified with chemicals or heat. Review with the students the changes that occur when natural rubber is heated. This process is called vulcanization. [The word vulcanization comes from the name of the Roman god of fire, Vulcan.]

Experiment 9:   Gooey glue   Date: _____

Objective: *In this experiment we will observe a change in properties as*
            two polymers are added together.

Hypothesis: *Liquid starch will change the polymer properties of white*
            Elmer's glue.   No difference will be observed between the
            two glues.

Materials:
    liquid laundry starch
    Elmer's white glue
    Elmer's blue glue (or another glue different from white glue)
    small jars (3-4)
    marker
    popsicle stick for stirring

Experiment:

Part I

1. Open the bottle of Elmer's white glue. Put a small amount on your fingertips.
   Note the color and consistency (sticky, dry, hard, soft) of the glue. Record
   your observations.

2. Now look carefully at the liquid starch. Pour a small amount out on your
   fingers or in a jar. Note the color and consistency of the starch. Record your
   observations.

3. Take one of the jars and put 4 tablespoons of water into it.

4. Note the level of water in the jar and draw a small line with a marker at the
   water level.

5. Add another 4 tablespoons of water and mark the water level with a
   marker.

6. Empty out the water.

Have the students state an objective and an hypothesis. Have the students read the experiment before writing these.

In this experiment the students will combine Elmer's white glue with liquid laundry starch. The liquid laundry starch will change the properties of the glue and create something like "silly putty," a soft maleable ball. The blue glue does not react in exactly the same manner. Have the students predict if there will be a difference between blue glue and white glue.

Because Elmer's glue is difficult to measure, steps 3-6 provide a way to measure a given amount of glue directly into the jar. The amount of starch added is not that important, but this is given as a guide. The time the glue stays in the starch is more critical-- more time in the starch results in a stiffer glue-starch "ball."

7. Fill the jar to the first mark with Elmer's glue.

8. Fill the jar to the second mark with liquid starch.

9. Mix the glue and the starch with the popsicle stick. Record any changes in consistency and color.

10. Take out the mixture in the jar and knead it with your fingers. Observe the consistency and color and record your results.

Results:

Observations for Elmer's white glue:

the glue is sticky, thick, with an odor

Observations for liquid starch:

the starch is thin, slippery, and light blue

Observations for mixture Elmer's white gue and equal amounts of liquid starch:

the properties of the glue change. the glue loses its stickyness and forms a clump.

The consistency of the glue will immediately change upon addition of the laundry starch, but it will still be sticky. The laundry starch needs to be "kneaded" into the glue.

Once enough laundry starch has been kneaded into the glue, the glue-starch ball can be removed from the jar.

Have the students note the change in the properties of the glue and help them think of ways to accurately describe the texture of the glue-starch ball:
- bouncy
- stretchy
- somewhat elastic like a rubber band
- blue/white in color

The mixture continues to get harder as the glue is allowed to react with the starch. Make more than one glue-starch ball and allow one to be mixed for a longer time, for comparison.

Part II

1. Now take another jar and fill it to the first mark with the Elmer's blue glue.

2. Now add liquid starch to the second level.

3. Mix.

4. Record your observations.

Results:

Observations for mixture of blue glue and liquid starch: _____

the blue glue becomes hardened and not rubbery like the white glue.

_____

_____

_____

Repeat the experiment using a different kind of glue. Elmer's blue glue works best, but any other brand of nonwhite glue can be used.

The consistency of the glue-starch mixture is different with clear or "blue" glues than with the white glue.

Conclusions:

Elmer's white glue changed from sticky to bouncy (stretch, like rubber) when liquid laundry starch was added.

Elmer's blue glue did not change in the same way as the white glue. The polymers that make up white glue are likely different from the polymers that make up blue glue.

Elmer's blue glue might be made of different molecules than Elmer's white glue.

Help the students write valid conclusions based on the data they have collected. Some examples are given.

Try to have the students relate the changes of the glue to the information given in the text.

Some conclusions can be inferred statements that are based on the data collected. For example, because the two glues behaved differently, it is possible that the chemical composition of each are different. Also, they have a different color and texture. However, this experiment did NOT prove that they are different chemically even though the experimental data suggest that this might be true. Discuss how additional investigation is needed to conclude anything about the chemical composition of the two types of glue.

Review

Define the following terms:

meros   *Greek word meaning "unit."*

polymer   *A word that means "many units."*

monomer   *A word that means "single unit."*

polyethylene   *"Many" ethylenes. A polymer used to make plastic.*

vulcanization   *A process to harden natural rubber that uses sulfur and heat.*

NOTES:

Chapter 10: Biological Polymers:
Protein and DNA

Time Required:

    Text reading - 1 hour
    Experimental - 30 minutes

Experimental setup:

    NONE

Additional Materials:

    Bread

Overall Objectives:

This chapter introduces two biological polymers: proteins and DNA. These are much more complicated molecules than those previously encountered. However, proteins and DNA are extremely important, so this chapter will serve as an introduction.

10.1 Introduction

The main points to emphasize are as follows:

- Proteins are polymers of amino acids.

- Protein polymers fold into different shapes.

- Protein shapes are important for their function.

- Many proteins are tiny molecular machines.

- DNA is a polymer of nucleic acids.

- DNA carries the genetic code and serves as the information library for each cell.

10.2 Proteins

Amino acids are the repeating units for proteins. All amino acids have the same basic structure, but have different "R" groups. Some amino acids are acidic, others are basic, and yet others have different properties. The "R" groups give amino acids these different properties.

10.3 Proteins are amino acid polymers

Protein polymers are connected through peptide bonds. This simply means that the carbonyl group hooks to the amine group. Amino acids are NOT hooked to each other via the "R" groups.

Short chains are called polypeptides and long chains are called proteins.

The shapes of proteins are important. Proteins fold into various shapes which are determined partly by the function that the protein performs.

The example given is kinesin (ki-nee-sin). Kinesin functions as a molecular delivery truck. It takes molecules from one place to another inside cells.

Kinesin has two "feet" (these are actually called heads), with which it moves along a microtubule "road." Microtubules are long strings of smaller proteins that make a large network of "roads" inside cells. Proteins get carried from place to place along these roads. Kinesin literally "walks" along this road one foot (head) at a time, carrying its cargo.

10.4 Protein polymers form special shapes

No matter how complicated the protein shape may look from the outside, it is just one folded-up chain on the inside. In the next figure, the picture on the left shows how human salivary amylase looks when all the atoms are shown. It is very compact, with little or no space between the atoms. The picture on the right is a simplified view that shows only the path of the protein chain, without all the extra atoms. It's still complicated, but by looking carefully one can see that there is only one continuous chain. (Notice also the coils. These are a common feature of almost all proteins.)

ven though the folded protein may look like a shapeless blob, it is actually folded very carefully to get the shape needed to carry out its job (or unction).

his picture shows a representative drawing of a kinesin molecule arrying a protein cargo. The "road" shown on the right is a helical array f tubulin molecules.

inesin is called a molecular motor because it moves things. There are many different kinds of motors inside living cells. Protein motors do lmost all of the work inside the cell. There are motors that cut, motors

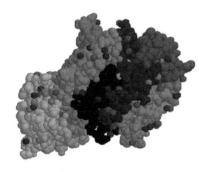
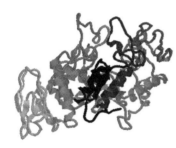

at build, and motors (like kinesin) that move things. For example, nyosin is a motor that looks much like kinesin but is used to power our nuscles. Dynein is another motor that powers tiny cilia that keep our ngs clear of dust.

10.5 Protein machines

Scientists still do not know all of the proteins inside cells and the roles they play. Many protein assemblies are very complex. Protein machines are very sophisticated motors, rotors, gears, pumps, and scissors. We have not yet learned to build structures with the precision and complexity of these remarkable molecular machines.

Recall that amylose is a starch found in bread and potatoes. In our mouths we have a protein machine called amylase that cuts amylose.

The names of amylose and amylase are very similar. Many enzymes (protein machines) are named after the molecules they work on. Amylase is the enzyme that breaks down amylose, the starch. Notice that the endings differ;" -ase" for the enzyme, "-ose" for the starch.

Enzymes are highly specific. That is, they work only on certain molecules. Amylase does not digest cellulose, only amylose. Cellulase, a different enzyme, digests cellulose. The name of an enzyme usually tells which molecule the enzyme works on.

The blue and green molecule (colored in student text) is the actual structure for human salivary amylase.

10.6 DNA

DNA is another biological polymer that is vitally important for all living things. The monomer units that make up DNA are more complicated than the amino acids that form proteins. However, DNA has only a few regular shapes.

10.7 DNA structure

DNA is made with nucleotides. These are composed of a ribose sugar and a base. The bases differ, but the sugars are the same for every unit.

There are 4 bases that make up most DNA. They are the following:

- Adenine A

- Guanine G

- Cytosine C

- Thymine T

When the two strands of the DNA molecule come together (see Section 10.8), the bases line up by forming pairs. Usually A pairs with T and G pairs with C in the ladder. Two strands of nucleic acid polymer make double-stranded DNA. DNA with only one strand does exist in nature, but it is chemically more susceptible to damage. Thus almost all DNA inside a cell is double stranded. The double-stranded form of DNA stores the genetic code.

In double-stranded DNA, the two strands of nucleic acids pair with the bases in the middle and the sugars on the outside. They then wrap around each other, much like a twisted ladder. These two wrapped polymers form a structure called a double helix since there are two helices wrapped around each other.

DNA carries the genetic code. The bases, A,C,T, and G code for proteins, which run the cell machinery. The bases can also code for things other than proteins, like signals (start signs and stop signs). DNA is like a big message that tells the cells which proteins to make, how much to make, when to make them, and when to stop. It tells the cells when to grow, when to divide, and when to die. There are many proteins involved in all of these functions, and scientists still do not understand how it all works!

10.8 Protein machines on DNA

One of the things that proteins do is copy DNA. This is done by a protein called DNA polymerase.

This is a large protein with lots of amino acids. When it binds to the DNA, it wraps itself around the chain and "holds" the DNA while it makes a copy.

Although DNA polymerases differ slightly between organisms, their basic shape is the same. They all have a "fingers" and a "thumb." The fingers open to admit new nucleotides, and the thumb holds the DNA in place. They also have a "palm" region between the fingers and thumb, which is responsible for the chemical reaction that actually adds new nucleotides.

10.9 Summary

Discuss with the students the main points of this chapter. There is a lot of information given in this chapter, and it is not important that the students understand everything presented. However, there are a few main points which the students should remember.

- Proteins and DNA are polymers that are inside every living thing. Proteins are amino-acid polymers, and DNA chains are made of nucleic acids and sugars.

- Proteins do all of the work inside our cells. They have a variety of functions which include moving molecules, synthesizing or making new molecules, and cutting and assembling molecules.

- DNA carries the genetic code. The genetic code is like a large library of information that tells the cells when to grow, when to divide, and what proteins to make.

NOTES:

Experiment 10:   Amylase action   Date: _____

Objective: *We will investigate the cutting action of proteins in our saliva.*

Hypothesis: *Saliva will cut the starch molecules in bread.   Iodine will not turn bread that has been soaked in saliva black.*

Materials:

> tincture of iodine [IODINE is poisonous. Do NOT eat.]
> bread
> timer
> wax paper
> marking pen

Experiment:

1. Break the bread into several small pieces.

2. Chew one piece for 30 seconds (use the timer), chew another piece for 1 minute, and a third piece for as long as possible (several minutes).

3. Each time after chewing the bread, spit it onto a piece of wax paper. Label with the marker the length of time the bread has been chewed.

3. Take a small piece of unchewed bread and place it next to the chewed pieces.

4. Add a drop of iodine to each piece of bread, chewed and unchewed.

5. Record your observations.

6. Take two more pieces of bread. Collect as much saliva from your mouth as you can (i.e., spit into a cup several times). Soak both pieces of bread in the saliva. Place one piece in the refrigerator and leave the other piece at room temperature. Let them soak for 30 minutes.

7. After 30 minutes add a drop of iodine to each. Record your results.

In this experiment the students will investigate the digestive process carried out by proteins in saliva.

Have the students read the experiment before writing an objective and hypothesis. Have them look back to Chapter 8 and ask them the following questions:

- • What molecule have we studied that is in bread?
  starch or amylose

- • What happens to food when we put it in our mouth?
  It begins to be broken down, digested.

- • What do you think happens to amylose in our mouth?
  It will be broken down, digested.

- • What do you expect iodine to do to unchewed bread?
  The iodine will turn the starch black.

- • What do you expect the iodine to do to chewed bread?
  The iodine will not turn it black.

- • Why?
  Amylose needs to be in a helical shape in order for iodine to turn it black. If amylose is broken apart, the helical shape is destroyed. Starch cannot turn it black if the helical shape is destroyed. Saliva has an enzyme, amylase, that breaks down amylose. Digestion of food begins in our mouth.

Based on these questions, have the students write a suitable objective and hypothesis. Some examples are given.

Results:

	Chewed Bread			Bread + Saliva 30 minutes	
30 seconds	1 minute	Several minutes	Un-chewed Bread	Refrigerated	Not Refrigerated

Conclusions:

Overall, the chewed bread was less black when iodine was added than the unchewed bread.

The refrigerated bread and the chewed bread were the same.

All of the pieces of bread looked the same. I could see no difference.

Have the students record their observations in the Results section. They should observe a decrease in the black color of the starch with the bread that has been chewed for longer time. Also, the refrigerated bread should be more black than the unrefrigerated bread.

Have the students write valid conclusions based on the data they have collected. Some examples are given.

Summarize the data and discuss with the students what is likely to have occurred:

1. The chewed bread and the bread with saliva at room temperature showed a decrease in the black color after iodine was added.
2. We know that bread contains starch (amylose).
3. We know that saliva has protein machines in it that begin the digestion of the food.
4. It is likely that the saliva contains a protein machine that breaks down the amylose in bread because of the color change with iodine.

These four statements are based both on data that has actually been collected (1) and information that has been gathered by other sources (2 and 3). The conclusion (4) is a likely conclusion, and most probably correct, but further data would need to be collected to prove that the concluding statement is true. Discuss how this investigation could lead to other experiments to prove the conclusion (i.e., a protein analysis to determine which proteins are in saliva). This is how real science works. Initial observations lead to additional experiments, which hopefully yield enough data to prove or disprove a given statement. Sometimes it takes years to collect all of the data, and sometimes enough data is never gathered. In these cases, the hypothesis remains unproven, and the most valid conclusions are only likely ones.

Review

Define the following terms:

protein   *A polymer of amino acids.*

amino acid   *A molecule that forms one unit of a protein chain.*

peptide bond *The chemical link between amino acids in a protein.*

kinesin   *A protein that walks along a molecular road and carries a cargo.*

DNA   *A polymer of nucleotides.*

nucleotide *A molecule that forms one unit in a DNA chain.*

double helix *Two strands of DNA polymers wrapped around each other.*

DNA polymerase *The protein machine that adds new nucleotides to a DNA chain.*

Draw a picture of kinesin.

What are the four bases that make up DNA?
Adenine, Thymine, Cytosine, and Guanine.

What are the symbols for the four bases that make up DNA?
A, T, C, and G.

NOTES:

Biology

Materials at a glance

Experiment 1	Experiment 2	Experiment 3	Experiment 4	Experiment 5	Experiment 6	Experiment 7	Experiment 8	Experiment 9	Experimen 10
items such as: rubber ball cotton ball tennis ball bannana apple paper stick paper clips rocks legos or building blocks	NONE: student worksheets only	(6) green leaves cardboard or stiff paper tape small jars marker	small jars (2) or more white carnation flowers food coloring	(2) small jars (4) or more pinto beans absorbant white paper plastic wrap clear tape (2) rubber bands	microscope with a 10X objective (3) eye droppers fresh pond water or _____ to order: Protozoa (Basic) set (13-1000) concavity culture slides (63-2935) (Carolina Biological Supply: www.carolina.com)	microscope with a 10X objective baker's yeast distilled water (3) eye droppers _____ to order: Congo Red stain (85-5363) concavity culture slides (63-2935) (Carolina Biological Supply: www.carolina.com)	tadpoples tadpole food small aquarium distilled water	caterpillar kit small cage _____ to order: butterfly kit (Carolina Biological Supply: www.carolina.com) or (Insect Lore www.insectlore.com)	clear glass or platic tank small plant: soil small bugs such as: worms ants beetles

Chapter 1: Living Creatures

Time Required:

Text reading - 1 hour
Experimental - 30 minutes

Experimental setup:

NONE

Additional Materials:

See materials list for Experiment 1.

Overall Objectives

This chapter introduces biology, the field of science concerned with the study of living things. In this chapter students will learn how living creatures are categorized. Because living creatures have unique features, the students will discover that it is often difficult to make exact categories for all living things. Often these categories get changed or become outdated. New classification schemes are constantly being tried and rejected.

1.1 The science of life

Explain to the students that there are many different disciplines of biology that deal with different aspects of living things. These disciplines include the following:

Molecular Biology : the study of the molecules, proteins, and DNA that make up living things.

Cell Biology: the study of the whole cells of living things.

Physiology : studies involving whole animal systems.

Genetics: studies concerned with the genetic information encoded in DNA.

Ecology: the study of living things and their interaction with the environment.

Botany: the study of plants.

Zoology: the study of animals.

1.2 Taxonomy

Discuss with the students that there are many different kinds of living things. Some are similar and some are very different. Have the students list some animals that are similar, like wolves and domestic dogs, and some animals that are different, like jellyfish and humans.

Point out to the students that living things differ from nonliving things because they are "alive" and they eventually die. Have the students think about what being "alive" means. Have them come up with their own definition of "living." Point out that nonliving things do not reproduce themselves, are not independently mobile, do not consume food or water, and do not die.

Taxonomy is that branch of science concerned with classifying living things. The term comes from the Greek word *taxis* meaning "arrangement" and *nomos* meaning "law." Carolus Linnaeus, a Swedish physician, began the systematic organization of living things into what is now called taxonomy. His system had only two kingdoms: plants and animals.

1.3 The kingdoms

Before discussing the various divisions, ask the students how they would classify living things. Ask them to make up their own groups. Answers will vary.

Because of the diversity of living things and because new information about known species continues to be discovered, it has been difficult to establish overall consensus on the classification of living things. In 1959, Cornell University Professor R.H. Whittaker, proposed a ive-kingdom system that is still used today. This is the system that s presented in this text. However, a four-kingdom system that only ecognizes four kingdoms -- Animalia, Plantae, Monera, and Virus -- has been proposed as well as an eight-kingdom system that recognizes the kingdoms Bacteria, Archaea, Archaeazoa, Protista, Chromista, Plantae, Fungi, and Animalia.   A three-domain system has also been proposed which would include the domains Bacteria, Archaea, and Eukarya.

Originally, the field of taxonomy was created to organize living things as a useful way to separate the various types of life into distinct categories for further study. Today, taxonomy is often a branch of evolutionary biology where an evolutionary connection is sought between certain species. For example, the distinction between the two domains Bacteria and Archaea is centered around difference in the ribosomal RNA sequences of species in these domains.

The first task in classifying living things is determining into which kingdom a given organism should be placed. Before the discovery of the microscope, all known living things were classified as either plants or animals. They were placed in these two categories based on their plant-like or animal-like characteristics. Today, an organism is placed into a given kingdom based primarily on the cell type of that organism. Cells are discussed in more detail in Chapter 2.

Although there are five kingdoms, there are not five different cell types. There are two basic cells types: prokaryotic and eukaryotic. (See Chapter 2.) Subsequently, there are two different types of eukaryotic cells: plant cells and animal cells. A diagram showing the division of kingdoms based on cell type follows:

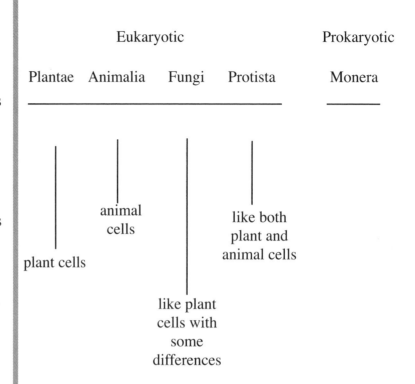

In spite of all of the classification difficulties, two main kingdoms stay consistent throughout all of the proposed classification schemes. These are the kingdoms, *Animalia* and *Plantae* (animals and plants).

The animal kingdom includes all animals. The common feature of all animals is the "animal" cell. This is covered in full detail in the next chapter. This is not to say that all animal cells are the same. In fact, animal cells have a wide variety of shapes, sizes, and functions. But all animal cells have certain features which place all animals in the animal kingdom.

Have the students think about what creatures might be in the kingdom *Animalia*. Have them list several creatures. If it is not immediately obvious that an organism is an animal, eliminate it from the other categories first.

For example, a student may say "shrimp," but maybe it's not clear that a shrimp is an animal.

> Is it a plant? (Plantae) *No.*
> Is it a bacteria? (Monera) *No.*
> Is it a single-celled organism or does it have both plant and animal like characteristics? (Protista) *No.*
> Is it a fungus? (Fungi) *No.*
> Then, it must be an animal in the kingdom Animalia.

The same is true for all plants that are in the plant kingdom. All plants have plant cells, the details of which are covered in the next chapter. Also, not all plant cells are identical: plant cells vary widely in shape, size, and function, but they all have similar basic features. Repeat the exercise above for plants. This may be trickier since a fungus can also look like a plant. Mushrooms, for example, are fungi, not plants. Use an encyclopedia or other resources if necessary.

The fungi originally were placed in the plant kingdom because they are sedentary like plants. However, fungi differ from plants in that they do not use the sun's energy for photosynthesis (see Chapter 3) and they differ structurally from plants. They are, therefore, in a kingdom of their own.

The fungi acquire their nutrients by absorption. They have special enzymes on the outside of their bodies that they use to break down food, which they then absorb. There are three basic classifications of fungi: decomposers, parasites, and symbionts. The decomposers live off nonliving organic matter such as fallen logs and animal corpses. The parasites absorb nutrients from a living host but can harm or kill the host. The symbionts acquire their food from a living host, but they are beneficial to the host they use.

The kingdoms Protista and Monera make up almost all of the microscopic organisms.

The cell type for Protista has similarities to both plant and animal cells. However, because they do not fit exclusively in either the plant or animal kingdom, they are given their own kingdom. These organisms are explained in more detail in Chapters 6 and 7.

The creatures in the kingdom Monera all have a particular cell type called a prokaryotic cell. (See Chapter 2.) Their cell shapes are diverse, but the most common shapes are rods, spheres, and spirals. *E. coli* is a type of bacteria that is rod-shaped and is found in our intestines. Pneumonia is caused by a sphere-shaped bacteria called pneumococcus.

1.4 Further classification

To further classify all living things, six additional categories are used. These differentiate between the various living things within a given kingdom.

The phylum, class, order, family, genus, and species are the names for these additional categories.

The phylum subdivides the kingdom into different groups. For the kingdom Animalia, some of the phylum divisions are

Phylum Chordata (those that have a backbone)
Phylum Mollusca (clams, mussels, and other bivalves)
Phylum Arthropoda (the insects)

The class divides each phylum of a given kingdom into more groups. Some of the classes for the phylum Chordata are

Class Amphibia (the frogs, toads, and newts)
Class Aves (the birds)
Class Mammalia (animals with mammary glands for nursing)
Class Pisces (the bony fishes)

1.5 Naming living things

The order divides the class, and the family divides the order. The family is further divided into the genus and species. This final classification gives each different creature a unique "two-name" designation. The first name is the genus name. *Genus* comes from the Latin word for "birth" or "origin" and is the generic name for a given organism. It is written with a capital letter and in italics. The second name (species name) is the specific name for that particular creature and it is written in lower case italics.

The example shown illustrates the different names for four different types of cats. It is not important that the students know all of these names, only that they understand how each is classified.

Point out that the scientific names of all living things are in either Latin or in Greek that has been "Latinized" by the addition of Latin endings. Linnaeus, although he spoke Swedish, used Latin to name living things. Latin was the universal language of scientists in his day, and he wrote most of his scientific work in Latin to make it available to other scholars. In general, the Latin or "Latinized" Greek name of a living thing often describes some unique feature of that organism. The name for the bobcat is *Felis rufa*. *Rufa* is Latin for "red," or "ruddy," since the bobcat has a reddish coat.

Not all names given to a specific organism reflect some scientific aspect of that creature. The scientist that discovers the organism has the right to give it its name. Some names reflect where the organism may have been found, and other names may be derived from the Greek myths or in honor of a person.

1.6 Summary

Review the following summary points of this chapter with the students:

• Biology is the study of living things. Review the difference between a living and a non-living thing. Discuss that taxonomy is a branch of biology that deals with classifying living things.

• The classification of living things begins with dividing them into various groups. Review the diagram with the students and point out the different groups. The largest groups are the kingdoms. Each kingdom is divided into the phylum, the phylum into the class, the class into the order, the order into the family, and the family into the genus and species. Review that the classification of a creature into a group depends on many things like its cell type, whether it lays eggs, whether or not it has a backbone, etc.

• Point out to the students why classifying living things is important. By knowing how organisms are different, or how they are similar, scientists can better understand how organisms live. For example, by observing the balancing behavior of a domestic cat on the edge of a narrow ledge, an understanding of how the mountain lion navigates the terrain of the Rockies may be possible. Also, observing the enmity between the neighborhood cat and the family dog may help explain the lack of cooperation between the lioness and the jackal.

NOTES:

Experiment: Putting things in order Date: _____

Objective: In this experiment we will try to organize a variety of objects into categories.

Materials:

Collect 20-40 different objects. Some suggestions are: rubber balls, oranges, cotton balls, banana, apple, paper, sticks, leaves, grass, etc.

Experiment:

1. Spread all of the objects on a table. Carefully look at each object and note some its characteristics. For example, some objects will be round or fuzzy; some will be edible, others not; some may be large, some small; and so on.

2. Record your observations for each item in the Results section.

3. Try to define "categories" for the objects. For example, some objects may be "hard," so one category can be called "Hard." Some objects may be "round," so another category can be "Round." Try to think of at least 4 or 5 different categories for your objects. Write the categories along the top of the graph in the Results section.

4. List the objects that fit into these categories. Note those objects that can fit into more than one category. Write these objects down more than once, if necessary, under all of the categories they will.

5. Take a look at each of the categories and each of the objects in those categories. Can you make "subcategories?" For example, some objects may all have the same color, so "Red" can be a subcategory. Some may be food items so, "Food" can be a subcategory. Pick three categories and try to list a couple of subcategories for each of these categories.

6. List the objects according to their category and subcategory.

In this experiment, the students will try to organize several different objects according to properties such as shape, color, or texture.

There are no exclusive "right" answers for this experiment, and the categories the students pick will vary.

Have the students collect a variety of objects. In order to have enough for several subcategories, pick 20-40 different objects.

Have them place the objects on the table and make careful observations. Discuss some features of the objects such as color, shape, and texture. Also, discuss any common uses such as those used as toys or those used as writing instruments.

Have the students write some notes on the objects they have collected. Have them briefly describe each object and list a few of its characteristics.

Next, have the students determine some overall categories into which the objects can be divided.   For example, marbles, cotton balls, and oranges are round, so "Round" could be a category. Basketballs, baseballs, and footballs are all balls, so another category could be "Types of Balls." Some items may fit into more than one category. Basketballs fit into both "Round" and "Types of Balls." Write those items that fit into more than one category in all of the categories they fit.

Next, have the students look at each category separately and choose three categories to further divide into subcategories. Decide how to further divide the items into subcategories.

Results:

Item	Characteristics
oranges	round, orange, food, sweet
grapes	oval, food, sweet, green
tennis ball	round, green, fuzzy
marshmallow	white, soft, sweet, shaped like a cylinder
cotton ball	round, white, fuzzy

Have the students record the characteristics of the various items. Help them be as descriptive as possible.

For example, oranges can be described as round, orange, sweet, food, living, etc. Tennis balls are round, fuzzy, yellow or green (or another color).

Help the students describe, in detail, several different items. Some sample items are listed.

Categories						
white	fuzzy	round	square	hard		
marshmallow	tennis ball	oranges				
cotton ball	cotton ball	tennis ball				
		cotton ball				

White		Fuzzy				Categories
ound	food	round	toys			Subcategories
cotton ball	marshmallow	cotton ball	tennis ball			

Have the students write the categories at the top of each column. USE PENCIL--they may want to change the categories as more items are written down.

Decide which items fit into each category and write those items in the column below the category name.

Pick one to three of the categories and divide them further into sub-categories. Try to pick categories so that all of the items are ultimately listed. If necessary, rename some of the general categories to better fit the items listed. Adjust the names of the categories and subcategories as needed so that each item is listed in a category and subcategory. It may be that not all of the items can be placed in a category and a subcategory.

This may be quite challenging. The point of this exercise is to illustrate the difficulty in trying to find a suitable organizational scheme for things with different characteristics.

Conclusions:

_____

_____

_____

_____

_____

_____

_____

Help the students write valid conclusions about the data they have collected. Some valid conclusions are as follows:

> "Both oranges and cotton balls are round."
> "Both cotton balls and marshmallows are white."
> "Tennis balls and cotton balls are both fuzzy."

Some conclusions that are not valid are as follows:

> "Both cotton balls and marshmallows are white. Marshmallows are sweet so cotton balls are sweet."

> "Tennis balls and cotton balls are both fuzzy. Tennis balls are bouncy so cotton balls are bouncy."

It is important to stick to the data that have been collected and not make statements about the items that are not true. It is obvious that marshmallows and cotton balls are both white, but it is not true that cotton balls are sweet. Two or more items having one or two things in common does not mean that all things are common between them. Discuss this observation with the students.

Discuss the difference between valid and invalid conclusions. A valid conclusion is a statement that generalizes the results of the experiment, but draws only from the data. It does not extend the results of the data to include things that haven't been observed nor does it connect results that should not be connected. An invalid conclusion is a statement that has not been proven by the data or a statement that connects the data in ways that are not valid. The example given is that marshmallows are sweet and white, but because cotton balls are white, it is invalid to say they are also sweet like marshmallows.

Review

What is taxonomy?   *The branch of biology concerned with classifying living things.*

List the five kingdoms.

Plantae	*Animalia*
Fungi	*Monera*
Protista	

List the other six categories for classifying living things.

phylum	*class*
order	*family*
genus	*species*

Which kingdom are dogs, cats, and frogs in?   *Animalia*

Which phylum are dogs, cats, and frogs in?   *Chordata*

Which class are frogs in?   *Amphibia*

Which order are dogs in?   *Carnivora*

Which family are cats in?   *Felidae*

What is the Latin name given to humans and what does it mean?

Homo sapiens. This means "man wise."

NOTES:

Chapter 2: Cells : The Building Blocks of Life

Time Required:

    Text reading - 1 hour
    Experimental - 1 hour

Experimental setup:

    NONE

Additional Materials:

    NONE

Overall Objectives

In this chapter the students will be introduced to cells, their proper names, and their structure. They should know that cells are the fundamental building blocks for all living things and that cells are highly complex and highly ordered.

2.1 Introduction

ALL living things are made of cells and there are no living things that are not made of cells. This unifying concept was not fully realized until the middle of the 19th century. Theodore Schwann and Matthais Schleiden, in separate publications in 1838 and 1839, presented the cell doctrine that all living things are composed of small units we call cells.

Today, we know much more about what cells look like, what they contain, and how they work. However, it is important to point out to the students that, although we know much more about cells than the early cell biologists of the 19th century, we are still very far from fully understanding them. Even the simplest cells are far more complex than ever imagined.

Cells, like nonliving things, are ultimately composed of atoms. The atoms combine to form molecules. Some of the molecules, like water, that are found in living things are also found in non-living things. But most molecules in living things are found ONLY in living things, like DNA and proteins.

Some organisms are composed of only one cell. But many organisms are made of lots of cells. These multicellular organisms are often composed of tissues that then form organs that fit together to form the whole organism.

2.2 The cell -- A small factory

The cell is like a small factory. There are many different molecules working together in a very systematic and orderly fashion. Even the simplest cells, the prokaryotic cells (see Section 2.4), that lack some of the features found in eukaryotic cells, are highly organized.

The illustration on student textbook page 12 shows some of the activities common to all cells.

1. Proteins and small molecules are moved in and out of cells.

2. Large molecules are manufactured from smaller molecules inside certain areas.

3. Molecules are transported from place to place within the cell.

4. Some molecules are stored for later use.

Point out to the students how the activities inside cells are coupled to each other. Ask the students to think about how a city works. Have them list some of the jobs that various people do in the city: i.e. postal workers carry the mail; sanitation personnel pick up the trash; etc. Now have the students think of just one job, say bringing milk to the grocery store. Have them think about all of the people and all of the tasks that must be done to get milk to the store. The cows need to be milked by the farmer, the milk needs to be processed by a dairy, the milk cartons need to be made by the factory, the milk cartons need to be delivered to the dairy, the dairy workers need to fill the milk cartons with milk, and so on. Now ask the students what would happen if one of those people did not do his job -- could the job get finished? Explain to the students that this is similar to how things work inside a cell.

The illustration on page 13 of the student text is a "key" for the cell factory illustration on page 12. The nucleic acids actually look like those in the drawing, but the large and small molecules are not actual molecules.

Page 13 of the student text explains some of the activities found in cells and the molecules that are involved.

Proteins do most of the work in cells. These are the cell's main machinery. They are responsible for transporting molecules within the cell and between separate cells. Proteins are also responsible for all of the molecule manufacturing, such as making other proteins and nucleic acids or making energy molecules. These proteins are called enzymes.

The nucleic acids are responsible for carrying the cell's "library." These molecules carry the information the cell needs to make new cells or other proteins in the cell.

All of the molecules in the cell work together to keep the cell functioning. Every molecule has a particular job. The cell knows how many molecules it has working at a particular time. Sometimes more molecules are made, and sometimes fewer of the same molecules are made. This depends largely on what the cell is doing and the surrounding environment. As the environment changes, the cell adjusts to these changes and may alter the manufacturing of certain molecules.

Point out to the students that, unlike nonliving things, cells die. The whole of a cell cannot be explained simply by the "sum of its parts" because even though all of the parts may still be around, cells die. A dead cell cannot come back to "life." Living cells can only come from other living cells and not simply from the machinery that composes them.

2.3 Types of cells

There are two basic cell types: prokaryotic cells and eukaryotic cells. All organisms are made of one of these two cell types.

Prokaryotes are the bacteria in the kingdom Monera. Prokaryotes lack a central membrane-bound nucleus that holds the genetic material, DNA.

Eukaryotes have a nucleus. Plants, animals, fungi, and protists are all composed of eukaryotic cells.

Eukaryotic cells are generally larger than prokaryotic cells with the total volume of a eukaryotic cell about a thousand times larger than that of prokaryote.

2.4 Prokaryotic cells

Prokaryotes are considered simple cells because they lack many features that eukaryotes possess.

For example,

1. Prokaryotes do not have a membrane-bound nucleus. (Eukaryotes do.)
2. Prokaryotes have a single DNA chromosome that is circular. (Eukaryotes have several linear chromosomes.)
3. The inside of the cell (cytoplasm) is almost devoid of structure. There is no cytoskeleton (no microtubules or actin as found in eukaryotes) and there are no organelles (as in eukaryotes -- see Section 2.7).
4. Energy production is a function of the whole cell and not the sole function of an organelle (as in eukaryotes).

Many prokaryotic cells have flagella or pili that move the organism. A flagellum is a long whip that is attached to a sophisticated motor that swirls the whip with great speed.

Pili are used by the cell for attaching to surfaces and to other cells. They are much longer than what is drawn in the illustration.

There are about 20,000 distinct bacteria known. In general, bacteria are tough and some can withstand extreme heat or extreme cold. Some bacteria are harmless and even beneficial to humans. *Escherichia coli* is a common bacterium found in our intestines that helps us digest food. Other bacteria can cause disease in humans and even death. Salmonella is a bacterium that causes food poisoning.

2.5 Plant cells

Plants are made of eukaryotic cells. Plant cells have both a membrane-bound nucleus and organelles.

Have the students carefully examine the illustration on page 16. It is not important that they remember all of the names for the organelles. Functions of some of the organelles are listed in Section 2.7. Have the students refer to this chart as they examine the cell.

Point out that plant cells have a cell wall. The cell wall gives plants the stiffness they need for standing upright. Plants also have chloroplasts. Chloroplasts are organelles that are used by the cell to make food through photosynthesis. (see Chapter 3.) These two features, cell walls and chloroplasts, make plant cells different from animal cells.

2.6 Animal cells

Animal cells have many of the same organelles as plant cells. Both plant and animal cells have mitochondria, a nucleus, ribosomes, and a cytoskeleton. The cytoskeleton is a network of microtubules and actin that is used for maintaining structural features of the cell and for transporting molecules from place to place within the cell.

As we have already seen, animal cells differ from plant cells in several important ways. First, animal cells do not have chloroplasts and do not use the sun's energy to make food. Animal cells also do not have cell walls, and they lack the central vacuole found in plant cells. So, although plant and animals cells have many similar features and are both eukaryotes, plants and animal cells are also different.

Point out to the students that these drawings represent idealized cells and that there are many different kinds of animal cells. We have bone cells, nerve cells, and skin cells, all with slightly different features. ALL of these cells are eukaryotic cells, but they are specialized to perform a particular task for our bodies.

2.7 Organelles

The table on page 18 of the student text shows functions for some of the organelles in eukaryotic cells. It is not important that the students memorize these functions, only that they understand that cells are highly organized and eukaryotes have organelles that perform particular tasks. Many organelles are membrane bound. That is they have a plasma membrane on the outside.

Have the students try to think of a living thing that isn't made of cells. Review with the students that all living things are made of cells.

Discuss with the students how cells are complex and function like small factories. Look at the illustration on page 12 of the student text and discuss briefly the various jobs that go on inside the cell. Ask the students what would happen to the cell if one or more of the jobs was not performed. For example, what would happen if the pores would not let molecules out (molecules would build up in the cell); or what would happen if no energy molecules were made (the cell would run out of energy); and so on.

2.8 Summary

Discuss the following main points of this chapter with the students:

Remind the students that eukaryotic cells have organelles but prokaryotic cells *do not*. This does not mean that prokaryotic cells are not complex, only that they do not have the same features as eukaryotic cells.

Ask the students to think about various organisms and what kind of organs they have. Then ask them what the organs are made of. Discuss with the students how each organ is important for the organism and performs some function.

For example, a cow has a stomach, and a stomach is made of stomach tissue. A stomach is used for digesting food. A cow cannot live without a stomach.

Point out that some organs are not essential for life (eyes) but that they are needed for a special purpose (seeing).

Experiment 2:   Inside the cell   Date: ——————————

Look at the drawings of the three types of cells from the text. Observe the similarities and the differences for the three different types of cells.

Write down some observations of things that are similar for all cell types:

All cells contain DNA.

All cells contain ribosomes.

All cells have something that holds them together, like a cell wall or plasma membrane.

Write down some observations that are different:

Prokaryotic cells do not have a nucleus.

Animal cells do not have a cell wall.

Plant cells contain chloroplasts, but animal cells do not.

Write down the function for each of the following:

Nucleus   *in eukaryotic cells; holds the DNA, and proteins needed to use the DNA, together.*

Mitochondria *organelles found in plant and animal cells that make energy.*

Chloroplasts *organelle found in plant cells that uses the sun's energy to make food.*

Cell wall *stiff outer membrane found in plant cells that makes the plant sturdy.*

Lysosome *the place where big molecules get broken down.*

Peroxisome *the place where poisons in the cell are removed.*

In this exercise the students will examine the similarities and differences between various cell types.

All cells share some common features. One such feature is DNA (deoxyribonucleic acid). DNA is often referred to as the genetic code. Almost every cell has DNA. The DNA in a cell contains many volumes of information.

Another component common to all cells are ribosomes. Ribosomes make proteins from RNA (ribonucleic acid). RNA is different from DNA but is still a nucleic acid. RNA is made as a copy of DNA and proteins are made by ribosomes that read the RNA copy. DNA->RNA->proteins. In living cells there are no known exceptions to this paradigm. Proteins are always made by using a copy of RNA and the RNA used to make proteins are always made by copying DNA.

How do animal cells differ from plant cells, and how do both plant and animal cells differ from bacterial cells?

List as many reasons as you can for the differences among bacteria, plants, and animals. Tell why you think their cells may differ.

Bacteria (have or don't have...)	Plants (have or don't have...)	Animals (have or don't have...)

Have the students look up bacteria in the encyclopedia.

Some facts about bacteria are as follows:

- They can be spherical, rod shaped, or spiral.
- They live in many different environments including soil, water, organic matter, and in the bodies of plants and animals.
- They are autotrophic (make their own food) or saprophytic (live on decaying matter) or parasitic (live off of a live host).
- Some can be beneficial and some can be harmful to humans

Plants have organs like animals and need many different types of cells. Have the students think about the different parts of a plant, like the leaves and roots, and discuss what their cells might need to do (i.e., root cells need to take up minerals from the soil, but are in the dirt so they are not green like leaves that need to use the chloroplasts for collecting light). Also, discuss how plant cells differ from animal cells. For example, plants don't have bones and they don't usually move, so they don't need muscles like some animals do. Have the students think of a variety of animals like deer, fish, and frogs. Discuss the differences and list why there are different types of cells in these creatures.

Without looking at your text, fill in the blanks with as many names for the structures in the cell as you can. Color the cell.

Is this an animal cell, a plant cell, or a prokaryotic cell? Write the cell type at the top.

Have the students fill in the blanks for the drawing on this page. Have them first try to do it without looking at the text. Have them color the organelles. The colors do not need to match those in the text.

As they fill in the blanks, discuss the functions of the various parts. Point out how the structures differ and, where possible, point out how the structure of the part matches its function. For example, the flagellum looks like a whip and is used as a whip for swimming. The cell membrane and cell wall are used to enclose the contents of the cell, so they are thin and extend around the outside.

Prokaryotic Cell

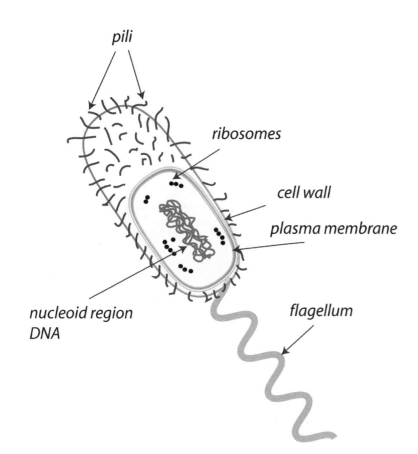

pili

ribosomes

cell wall

plasma membrane

nucleoid region
DNA

flagellum

Without looking at your text, try to fill in the names as many of the structures as you can.

Is this an animal cell, a plant cell, or a prokaryotic cell? Write the type of cell at the top.

Have the students fill in the blanks for the drawing on this page. Have them first try to do it without looking at the text. Have them color the organelles. The colors do not need to match those in the text.

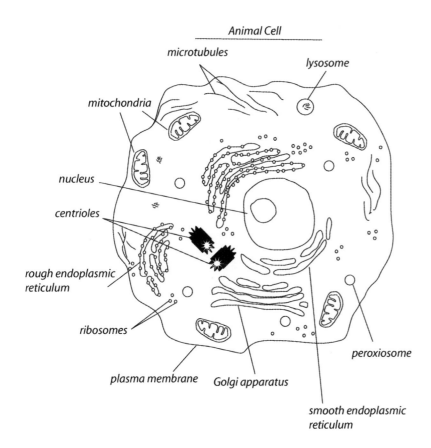

Animal Cell

microtubules

lysosome

mitochondria

nucleus

centrioles

rough endoplasmic reticulum

ribosomes

plasma membrane   Golgi apparatus

peroxiosome

smooth endoplasmic reticulum

Without looking at your text, fill in the blanks with the names for as many names of the structures in the cell as you can. Color the cell.

Is this an animal cell, a plant cell, or a prokaryotic cell? Write the type of cell at the top.

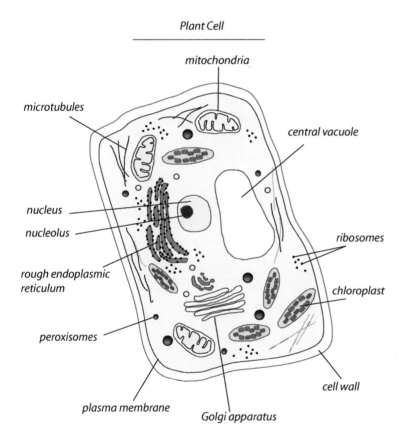

Plant Cell

mitochondria

microtubules

central vacuole

nucleus

nucleolus

ribosomes

rough endoplasmic reticulum

chloroplast

peroxisomes

cell wall

plasma membrane

Golgi apparatus

Have the students fill in the blanks for the drawing on this page. Have them first try to do it without looking at the text. Have them color the organelles. The colors do not need to match those in the text.

Conclusions:

_____

_____

_____

_____

_____

_____

_____

_____

_____

_____

_____

_____

Help the student write some conclusions about cells based on what they have learned in this chapter.

Some examples include the following:

"Bacteria and animal cells are very different"

"Animals are different from plants and have different types of cells. "

"Plants don't have skeletons like animals."

Review

Answer the following questions:

What are cells made of? *Cells are made of a highly organized arrangement of atoms and molecules.*

What are tissues made of? *Tissues are made of cells.*

What are organs made of? *Organs are made of tissues.*

Define the following terms:

prokaryote *The simplest type of cell; Bacteria is a prokaryotes.*

eukaryote *Cell with a nucleus; Plants and animals are eukaryotes.*

organelle *Specialized sacks that function as tiny "organs" inside cells.*

Name some organelles found in plant or animal cells:

chloroplast   *mitochondria*

nucleus   *peroxisome*

Golgi apparatus   *lysosome*

What does a flagellum do? *A flagellum is used by some organisms for movement.*

Where are chloroplasts mostly found? *Chloroplasts are found mostly in plants.*

What are mitochondria for? *Mitochondria are used by the cell to make energy.*

NOTES:

Chapter 3: Cells : Photosynthesis

Time Required:

      Text reading - 1 hour
      Experimental - 1 hour

Experimental setup:

      NONE

Additional Materials:

      Fresh green leaves (6)

Overall Objectives

In this chapter the students will be introduced to photosynthesis. Photosynthesis is the process by which plants harvest the sun's energy to make food.

3.1 Introduction

Ask the students how plants eat. Have the students look at the picture in the student text and ask them why plants don't eat cheeseburgers. Answers will vary, but try to get them to understand that plants can't eat cheeseburgers because plants don't have the following, among other things:

    teeth
    mouth
    stomach
    saliva
    fast food restaurants

Explain that plants are photosynthetic. That is they use the sun's energy to make their own food. Not all plants are solely photosynthetic. There are a few carnivorous and parasitic plants that obtain additional nutrients by nonphotosynthetic means.

For example, mistletoes and dodders are parasitic plants that obtain nutrients from other photosynthetic, food-making plants. These plants wrap long vines around the stems of photosynthetic plants and penetrate the stems with tiny root-like appendages. In this way, they obtain water, sugar, and other nutrients from the host.

There are about 450 carnivorous plants. The best-known examples are the Venus flytrap, sundews, and pitcher plants. These plants obtain additional nutrients by capturing insects. These plants can use photosynthesis and survive without capturing insects, but they grow faster and are greener when they are supplied with insects.

3.2 Chloroplasts

Photosynthesis occurs in specialized organelles called chloroplasts. The actual biochemical steps are quite complicated and beyond the scope of this level. However, a schematic outline is presented later which shows the essential steps.

The overall reaction is the following:

carbon dioxide (CO_2) + water (H_2O) + light = sugar + oxygen (O_2)

Carbon dioxide enters, and oxygen exits, the leaves of photosynthetic plants through small holes called stomata. These pores can open and close.

Chlorophyll molecules "pick up" the light energy and transfer this energy to other molecules in a series of reactions that ultimately produces sugar molecules. This is an example of "light energy" being converted into "chemical energy." The details of this process are not important at this point.

The chlorophyll molecules are located in the thylakoid. Stacked thylakoids form the granum.

It is hard to overemphasize the importance of photosynthesis to all living things. All creatures need a source of energy or they will die. Plants use photosynthesis to make their food and they get energy from the sun. We, and all other animals, get our energy by eating plants or by eating other animals that eat plants. The sun's energy is ultimately the source of energy for all living things. Plants put this energy into a form usable by animals like ourselves.

3.3 Why plants have leaves

Leaves are the main organ for carrying out photosynthesis in plants. Many leaves are broad which enables them to collect as much light as possible.

Discuss with the students how a broad leaf would pick up lots of light and a small leaf would pick up less light. (The bigger and broader the leaf, the more exposure to the sun it has.) If possible, have the students collect a few varieties of leaves from their yard or neighborhood and discuss with them the various shapes you find. Also show the students how the leaves can pick up sunlight from all directions by being attached to the tree at different angles. You can do this by simply looking at a tree and trying to find out which leaves have direct sunlight hitting them and then later in the day show them that different leaves have direct sunlight.

Evergreen trees have a different type of leaf. The leaves on evergreen trees are narrow and thin. Evergreen trees have narrow leaves because these trees often live in areas with little water. These leaves have a thick outer coating, called a cuticle, that covers the leaf and reduces water loss. These narrow leaves collect less sunlight, but the narrow shape also makes them less likely to lose water. The cuticle and capacity to "hold" water are the features that enable evergreen trees to withstand cold winter temperatures and dry weather.

3.4 Photosynthesis in other organisms

Land plants are not the only organisms that carry out photosynthesis. Seaweed and microscopic algae are usually classified in the kingdom Protista. However, some of the multicellular varieties of algae, like red algae, are still placed in the plant kingdom or in the "red plant kingdom."

Algae use photosynthesis to make food just as green land plants do. Many algae have chlorophylls of slightly different molecular form in addition to the chlorophyll found in land plants. These chlorophylls give algae their characteristic red or brown coloration.

Other organisms that use photosynthesis to make food include the cyanobacteria and several different protists. (see Chapter 6.)

Cyanobacteria were once considered algae, but they are now known to be prokaryotes and are classified in the kingdom Monera. Cyanobacteri contain chlorophyll like green land plants and also have thylakoids. They can exist as single organisms or in colonies. "Pond scum" is typically made of several different varieties of cyanobacteria.

3.5 Summary

In summary, discuss with the students the following main points from this chapter:

Ask the students how plants get their food (most by photosynthesis, a few as parasites, and some by eating insects).

Ask the students to describe in as much detail as they can what photosynthesis is. Have them look at the picture of the chloroplast.

Ask the student to explain which parts of a plant participate in photosynthesis.

stems: yes	flower buds: yes	fruit: yes some
leaves: yes	roots: not directly	

NOTES:

Experiment 3:   Take away the light   Date:_____

Objective: *In this experiment we will remove the sunlight from several plant leaves and observe the changes over many days.   We will compare these changes to several other leaves that have been removed from the plant but exposed to light and supplied with water.   This will allow us to observe if light and water are sufficient to keep the plant leaves alive.*

Hypothesis:_____

_____

_____

Materials:

   lightweight cardboard or construction paper
   tape
   plant with flat leaves (6)
   small jars
   marker

Experiment:

1. Take some cardboard or construction paper and cut it into squares large enough to cover the front and back of a leaf.

2. We will test six different leaves. Two of the leaves will be left on the plant (attached) and four leaves will be removed from the plant (unattached).

3. Of the two attached leaves one will be covered and the other uncovered. The four unattached leaves will be tested as follows: covered in water, uncovered in water, uncovered out of water, and covered out of water.

4. With the marker, label the leaves in the following manner:

   Leaf 1: UA- uncovered, attached
   Leaf 2: CA- covered, attached
   Leaf 3: UUW- uncovered, unattached, in water
   Leaf 4: CUW- covered, unattached, in water
   Leaf 5: UU- uncovered, unattached (no water)
   Leaf 6: CU- covered, unattached (no water)

In this experiment the students will examine the effects of removing light from the leaves of a photosynthetic plant.

Have the students first read the experiment through to determine what is being investigated. Discuss with the students the possible outcomes of each of the leaves. Ask the students the following questions before writing the hypothesis:

1. What do you think will happen with Leaf 1? It is uncovered but not attached to the plant. It can get sunlight, but it does not have water.
2. What will happen to Leaf 2? It is covered but still on the plant. This means it cannot have any sunlight, but it does get water and other nutrients from the rest of the plant.
3. What will happen to Leaf 3? It is uncovered (will get sunlight), not attached to the plant (no additional nutrients), but placed in water (so it will receive water).
4. What will happen to Leaf 4? It is covered (will not get sunlight) it is unattached (will not get additional nutrients), but it will get water.
5. What will happen to Leaf 5? It is uncovered (will get sunlight), but it has no water or nutrients.
6. What will happen to Leaf 6? It is covered (will get no sunlight), and it will not get any water or additional nutrients.

Have the students guess which leaves will die first, which will not die at all, and which may survive a short time. Help them write a suitable hypothesis based on this discussion. Some examples are the following:

   "All of the leaves not in water will die."
   "Only the leaves without sunlight will die."
   "Only leaf 6 will die.

5. Take two small jars and fill them with water. Take the two leaves that will be placed in the water and prop them in the jars, keeping the stems submerged. Check the water level every day over the course of the experiment to make sure there is enough water in the jars.

6. Observe the changes to the leaves daily by carefully removing the cardboard and then retaping it and recording your observations.

Results:
Observations:

	UA	CA	UUW	CUW	UU	CU
Day 1						
Day 2						
Day 3						
Day 4						
Day 5						
Day 6						
Day 7						
Day 8						
Day 9						
Day 10						

The results for this experiment may vary depending on the type of plant that is used. Tree leaves can also be used.

Two of the leaves in this experiment are "controls." The leaf that is attached and uncovered is a positive control (Leaf 1). This leaf should remain healthy throughout the course of the experiment unless something happens to the plant. The leaf that is covered and unattached and without water is a negative control (Leaf 6). This leaf should die first. Discuss the use of controls with the students.

Positive controls help the investigator determine if the experimental setup is working. Negative controls tell the investigator when the desired effects of the experiment have indeed occurred. Both types of controls are useful for making sure the experimental results are valid. In other words, if the positive control did not work (the leaf dies on the plant), then when the other leaves die, it cannot be concluded that the leaves died because of the changes in the experiment. Likewise, the negative control should be a negative result (the leaf should die without water or sunlight) to prove that the other samples survive or die accordingly. If the negative control survives, it is an indication that something else is happening--the leaves are especially tough, the experiment needs more time, a plastic plant was used instead of a real one so the leaves never die. (Anything is possible.) Positive and negative controls give the experimenter the boundaries of the experiment and allow him/her to make valid conclusions about the samples in between.

Have the students record the results in the boxes. Have them write any observation they see. Short one or two word descriptions like, "green," "green with some brown," "mostly brown," and "wrinkled," are fine.

Conclusions:

_____

_____

_____

_____

_____

_____

Have the students write conclusions based on their results. Help them write accurate and valid conclusions.

For example,

"Leaf 1 survived for one week."

"Leaf 2 did not survive past two days."

"Leaf 3 survived for one week. Leaf 3 needs only sunlight and water to live one week unattached from the plant."

"All of the leaves without sunlight turned yellow-brown, but did not die."

Have the students discuss what they learned. Is it true that water and sunlight alone are sufficient for the survival of a detached leaf? How about for a leaf that remains attached, but lacks water and sunlight--are water and sunlight required for this leaf to survive?

Review

Define the following terms:

photosynthesis: *Photo means "light" and synthesis means "to make." Photosynthesis is the process used by plants to make food using sunlight.*

chloroplast: *Chloroplasts are the tiny organelles inside the leaves of plants where photosynthesis occurs.*

chlorophyll: *Chlorophylls are the molecules inside chloroplasts that "capture" the sun's energy for photosynthesis.*

conifer: *A conifer is an evergreen tree. It has thin needlelike leaves.*

algae: *A protozoan that uses photosynthesis like land plants to make food.*

cyanobacteria: *Bacteria that use photosynthesis to make food.*

How do most green plants get their food? Do they eat cheeseburgers?

Most land plants get their food using photosynthesis. They never eat cheeseburgers.

NOTES:

Chapter 4: Parts of a Plant

Time Required:

     Text reading -- 1 hour
     Experimental -- 1 hour

Experimental setup:

     NONE

Additional Materials:

     Two or more fresh white carnations

Overall Objectives

In this chapter the students will learn the features that make up the majority of land plants. The students should be able to list the parts of flowering plants.

4.1 Introduction

Plants are the main food producers on the earth. There are more than 250,000 different land plants known, with an additional 150,000 plants not found on land. Plants grow in most areas except where there is extreme hot or cold such as at the north and south poles and the driest parts of the desert. Discuss with the students the importance of plants. Discuss with them how plants provide food for all living things. Have them think of what they eat, and have them try to think of something they eat that doesn't come from plants. For example, they may say "marshmallows" as something they eat that's not a plant. However, marshmallows are made mostly of sugar, and sugar comes from sugar cane -- a plant!

Discuss with the students the many different kinds of plants that we use for food. Ask them to identify which parts they think we eat. Is a cherry a flower? Is an asparagus a leaf? Is an ear of corn a root?

Here are some examples:

Cherries, apples, pears, oranges, and avocados are all fruit.
Lettuce, cabbage, spinach, and kale are all leaves.
Celery, asparagus, and broccoli are all stems and leaves.
Artichokes are flowers.
Peas, corn, and beans are all seeds.

Discuss with the students that we don't eat all types of plants and that some plants are even poisonous.

4.2 How plants live

Plants are designed to live in dirt and in the air.

Plants have specialized tissues that allow them to absorb nutrients from the earth's soil and light, and water from the earth's atmosphere. As we saw in Chapter 3, the leaves of a land plant are able to "capture" the sun's energy to make food. Leaves are also designed to exchange oxygen and carbon dioxide from the surrounding air. The roots of a plant are designed to take in nitrogen, minerals, and water from the soil.

There are two main parts common to all land plants: the shoot system and the root system. The shoot system exists above the soil and consists of the stems, leaves, and, in flowering plants, the flowers. The root system is that part of the plant that exists below the surface of the soil.

The components that make up these systems are called organs. The organs of plants are made of many cells which perform particular tasks. For example, in the vascular tissue of vascular plants, there are different types of cells. Some cells form the epidermis, which covers the outer areas. Some form the cortex, which is just inside the epidermis. On the leaves, there are guard cells that open and close to allow air and moisture in.

All of the organs work together to maintain the life of the plant. The stem supports the leaves and flowers, transports water and minerals from the roots, and even stores food. The roots anchor the plant to the surface of the soil, absorb water and minerals from the soil, and store food. The leaves make food with photosynthesis and export the food to the rest of the plant. When any one of these organs is cut off from the rest of the plant, it does not easily survive on its own.

4.3 Parts of a plant: roots

The root system serves the following two main functions:

1. Anchorage to the soil
2. Absorption of nutrients from the soil

Some roots, especially the roots of sugar beets, carrots, and sweet potatoes, are also food storage organs for the plant.

There are two main types of root systems: the taproot system and the fibrous root system.

The taproot system has a central root that goes straight down, deep into the soil. Smaller roots branch off from this central root and are called feeder roots. The taproots of many desert plants extend several meters into the soil to reach deep sources of water.

Fibrous roots are different than taproots in that there is no central root but, instead, several main roots that extend downward with smaller roots extending from them. These form a dense mass. Grasses have this kind of root system, and the many small roots help secure grasses firmly in the soil.

Roots have special tissues which allow the absorption of minerals and water from the soil. Roots have a large surface area which aids in the absorption of water and minerals. Most of the absorption occurs at the tip of the root where the outer surface is thin and where there are many root hairs. The root hairs (small roots branching out from the larger roots) are responsible for most of the surface area of roots.

The shoot system of plants consists of the stems, leaves, and flowers.

4.4 Parts of a plant: stems

The stems of a plant are usually long and contain nodes and buds. Some stems are horizontal and some stand erect. Some stems are creeping stems, and some are vines that climb other plants or solid structures.

Stems contain two main tissues: xylem and phloem. These two tissues are responsible for transporting food, minerals, water, and other nutrients from the leaves to the roots and back up from the roots to the leaves.

The xylem and phloem can be arranged in concentric rings centering the core tissue called the pith. The xylem and phloem can also be intermixed, but still surrounding the pith. This varies depending on the type of plant. The pith can also extend rays which radiate from the central core. Food storage is the principle function of the pith. The xylem mainly transports minerals from the roots to the leaves at a rate of about 15 meters per hour for most plants. The fluid in the xylem rises up against gravity by capillary action without the use of molecular motors or pumps. The capillary action is created by vaporation of water from the leaves. As water evaporates from the eaves, a negative tension or pressure pulls the water up from below.

he transport of sugars in the phloem works by a different mechanism han the transport of minerals in the xylem. The phloem sap moves hrough a series of sieve tubes connected to each other end to end. The ugar is transported with small protein pumps that pump the sugar into he phloem tissue.

.5 Parts of a plant: flowers

lowers are the reproducing organ of flowering plants.

lowers form from the shoot and contain four floral organs called the epals, petals, stamens, and carpels. Flowers that contain all four floral rgans are called complete flowers. Some flowers, like those on most rasses, lack petals and are referred to as incomplete flowers.

he stamen is the "male" part of the flower, and the carpel is the female" part. At the tip of the stamen is the anther which releases ollen grains. Pollen is collected at the tip of the carpel and travels down he pollen tube into the base where the eggs are housed inside the ovary. he pollen fertilizes the egg which gives rise to an embryo and develops nto the seed.

nce the pollen grains fertilize the eggs inside the ovary, the flower dies. fruit develops which holds a single seed, or several seeds, depending n the species. When the fruit falls off the plant, it can be carried to ther places by the wind or animals. If the conditions are right, the seeds ill grow into a new plant.

4.6 Summary

Discuss with the students the summary statements listed on page 31 of the student text.

Experiment 4:   **Colorful flowers**   Date:_____

Objective: In this experiment we will observe the flow of water from the
base of a stem to the flower.

Hypothesis: _____

_____

Materials: _____

small jars
several white carnation flowers (2 or more)
food coloring

Experiment:

1. Take several of the small jars, add water and several drops of food coloring.

2. Trim the ends of one carnation stem and place it in the colored water.

3. Watch the petals of the carnation and record any color changes observed.

4. Take out the carnation and cut a small slice of the stem off from the bottom. Try to identify the xylem and the phloem. Draw a picture of what you see in the Results section. Cut the carnation flower lengthwise. Try to identify the parts of the flower.

5. Take one stem and slice it about halfway towards the flower lengthwise with a knife. (Have an adult help you.) Stick one end in a solution of colored water and place the other end in a different color of water. Let the carnation soak up the colored water until the petals begin to change color. Draw a picture of what you observe in the Results section.

In this experiment the students will observe the transport of water through the xylem of a carnation stem. Have the students read the experiment in its entirety before writing the hypothesis.

Two variations of transport will be investigated. First, simple transport up the stem of the carnation will be examined. This experiment serves to establish a control so that predictions on the second variation can be made. The transport observed in this first variation should result in petals with single colors. This experiment demonstrates that colored water is indeed transported up the stem to the petals of the flower.

In the second variation, the stem is split lengthwise about halfway to the flower. Each end is placed in a jar with different-colored water.

Have the student predict what will happen in both cases. Ask the following questions:

1. Will the colored water travel to the petals of the flower?
2. Will two different colors travel up to the flower in the second experiment?
3. Will the petals on the flower from the second experiment be a single color, or will the petals have two colors?
4. Do you think the colored water will travel straight in the second experiment, or will the colors mix in the stem? How could we tell which is happening?

Have the students write a hypothesis bases on their answers to these questions. For example:

" The colored water will not travel to the flower."

"The split stem will not allow any colored water to travel to the flower."

" The split stem will give two colors in the petals."

esults:

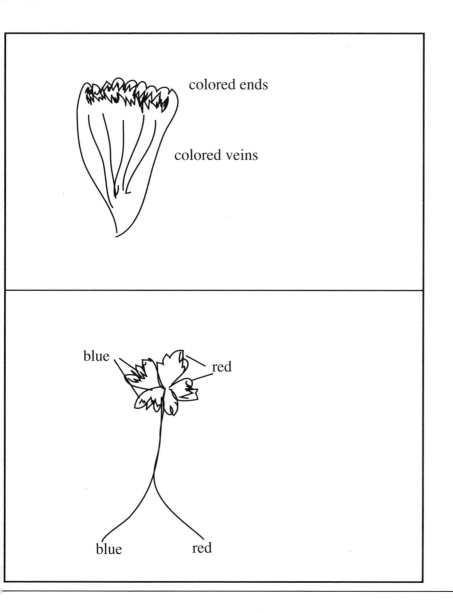

colored ends

colored veins

blue   red

blue   red

Have the students record their results. Petals can be removed from the flower and taped into the boxes. The petals will not be uniformly colored, but will have a dark strip of color at the very end. If enough time is allowed, the veins in the petal will also turn colors.

The split carnation will result in a flower with two colors split in the middle. The colored water travels up the split stem and colors only the petals on the same side. The colors do not mix and the split stem does not prevent the colored water from being transported.

VARIATIONS (optional)

If additional carnations are available, some additional questions can be investigated.

What happens if a carnation is allowed to soak in one color and then transferred to a different color? Do the colors blend at the tip of the petals or are the petals striped?

What happens if one carnation is left out for a short time without any water and another is placed in water for the same amount of time. Will one "drink" water faster than the other?

What happens if some of the petals are removed from the flower. Will the remaining petals be darker in color or color faster? Compare two flowers in the same-colored water solution. Remove several petals from one flower and compare the petal colors for each flower.

Conclusions:

_____

_____

_____

_____

_____

_____

_____

Help the students write valid conclusions based on their results:

Some examples are as follows:

> *"The colored water travels through the stem to the petals."*
> *"The colored water did not mix in the split stem."*
> *"The splitting of the stem did not prevent the colored water from traveling to the petals."*

eview

efine the following terms:

1. xylem: *a tissue found in the stems of plants used to move water and minerals up from the roots*

2. phloem: *a tissue found in the stems of plants used to move food down to the roots*

3. pith: *the tissue found in the center of a stem used for food storage*

4. pollen: *small grains found in flowers used to make seeds*

5. stamen: *the part of the flower that holds the anther where the pollen is made*

6. ovary: *the base of the carpel where the egg is housed*

ame the four main parts of a plant:

1. *stems*

2. *roots*

3. *leaves*

4. *flowers*

ame two types of roots:

1. *fibrous roots*

2. *taproots*

NOTES:

Chapter 5: How A Plant Grows

Time Required:

> Text reading - 1 hour
> Experimental - 1 hour

Experimental setup:

> NONE

Additional Materials:

> Two or more fresh white carnations

Overall Objectives

In this chapter the students will examine how plants grow from a seed to a full-sized plant. This chapter focuses only on the life cycle of flowering plants. Only flowering plants have seeds. Other plants, such as ferns, reproduce with spores.

5.1 Introduction

Discuss with the students how plants grow. Ask them if they can think of a plant that does not start out as a seed. Explain to the students that although not every plant has flowers, every plant starts off as a seed.

5.2 Flowers, fruits, and seeds

All flowering plants begin life as tiny seeds. The seeds of *flowering* plants are formed inside the flower. There are many different kinds of flowers. Some flowers are very small and are difficult to see with the unaided eye, like the flowers of duckweed. Some flowers are very large, like the Rafflesia, which grows on the floor of dark tropical forests and gets as large as 3 or 4 feet in diameter.

Following fertilization with pollen, the flower produces a fruit at its base. The fruit protects the seed and may help in the germination of the seed. Simple fruits contain one ovary at the end of one carpel (see Chapter 4, section 4.5) and produce one seed. The avocado is an example of a simple fruit containing one seed. Aggregate fruits, such as strawberries, blackberries, and raspberries have flowers with many carpels and many ovaries resulting in many seeds bunched together. Multiple fruits differ slightly from aggregate fruits and are formed by the individual ovaries of several flowers which bunch together to make one fruit. A pineapple is an example of a multiple fruit.

5.3 The seed

Seeds come in different shapes and sizes. Some seeds, like the maple seed and dandelion seed, are designed to be carried by the wind. They have propeller-shaped fruit or tufts of hairs that help them float in the wind. Other seeds are designed to be carried away by animals like those that are in burrs. Have the students think about various seeds and their shapes and discuss whether the seeds are carried away by wind or animals.

Before the seed is released, a small embryo or baby plant develops. It is housed inside the seed and gets food from the cotyledons (cot-ə-lē´-dons). The cotyledons are the fleshy part of the seed. Both the embryo and cotyledons are encased in a tough outer coating called the seed coat. The seed coat protects the seed from harm. Seed coats can be smooth, like that of a bean, or rough and sculptured, like that of a peach or plum seed.

5.4 The seedling

When the conditions are right and there is enough moisture, the seed will begin to germinate. The first indication of germination is swelling of the seed with water. First, a small root emerges called the radicle. The radicle grows downward into the soil to ensure that the germinating seed will have enough water and nutrients for full growth. In the next step, for seeds such as beans, peas, castor beans, and onions, a small hook is formed from the radicle which helps the bean push through the soil. The new stem now straightens and, as sunlight hits the seedling, new leaves emerge and begin making food by photosynthesis. These new leaves are called foliage leaves.

Not all seeds germinate in exactly the same way. A wheat grain, for example, does not form a hook for pushing through the soil. Instead, the stem emerges as a straight shoot.

The cotyledons are the food reserves for the seed. Once photosynthesis has begun, the cotyledons are no longer needed. They wither and fall away from the new seedling.

5.5 Signals for plant growth

There are many different chemical signals that tell plants how to grow. In general, these signals are called tropisms. Tropisms are anything that cause a plant to turn toward a stimulus. Tropism comes from the Greek word *tropos* which means "turn."

There are three main tropisms that tell plants where to grow: phototropism, gravitropism, and thigmotropism.

Photo mean "light," so phototropism means "turning toward light." This is the signal plants get from sunlight. Plants will always grow toward sunlight.

Gravitropism is "turning toward gravity." Roots exhibit positive gravitropism, and shoots exhibit negative gravitropism. Roots grow in the direction of gravity, and shoots grow opposite the direction of gravity.

Thigmo means "touch," so thigmotropism means "turning toward touch." Climbing vines exhibit this type of tropism. A vine will grow straight until it contacts another surface. This contact stimulates the vine to coil around the surface.

Point out the various types of stimuli that cause plants to grow. Discuss with the students how these are "signals," much like stop signs and traffic lights that tell drivers where to turn and where not to turn, when to go and when to stop.

5.6 Plant nutrition

Although plants make all of their own food with photosynthesis, they require certain mineral nutrients for proper growth. Mineral nutrients are absorbed by the roots from the soil.

There are 17 essential mineral nutrients that are required for healthy plant growth. These include phosphorus, calcium, magnesium, potassium, sulfur, nitrogen, iron, boron, manganese, zinc, copper, and nickel, to name a few. Some mineral nutrients are required in large amounts, like nitrogen and calcium, but others are only needed in small quantities, like zinc and copper.

Mineral deficiencies in plants are usually obvious by the change in leaf color or overall growth of the plant. A tomato plant that is deficient in magnesium, for example, will have yellow leaves.

The mineral nutrients are involved in many of the biochemical mechanisms of the plant. For example, magnesium is needed for chlorophyll production and calcium is required for maintaining membrane structure. Phosphorus is needed for cell membranes and for making DNA; and nitrogen is needed for making proteins and DNA.

5.7 The life cycle of flowering plants

The figure on page 37 of the student text summarizes the life cycle of flowering plants.

The students should be familiar with each of the steps: flower to seed-containing fruit, fruit to germinating seed, seed to seedling, seedling to young plant, and finally, young plant to mature, flowering plant.

NOTES:

It should be pointed out to the students that there are other plants that do not make seeds or have flowers and that reproduce by other means. For example, ferns and horsetails are seedless plants that reproduce using spores. Mosses are a different kind of seedless plant that use spores for reproduction.

New plants can also be grown from existing plants. "Cuttings" can be removed from some plants and, when placed in water, new roots will grow. Some plants also put out thin extended stems which will sprout a new baby plant and roots. Thus other mechanisms of reproduction can be found in the plant kingdom.

5.8 Summary

Discuss with the students the main points to remember from this chapter listed on page 38.

Experiment 5: Which way is down?   Date: _____

Objective: *In this experiment we will observe the growth of several*
            bean seeds. We will examine the direction the roots
            and stems grow.

Hypothesis: _____

            _____

Materials:

    small jars (2)
    several pinto beans
    absorbent white paper
    plastic wrap
    clear tape
    two rubber bands

Experiment:

1. Cut strips of white paper the width of the jars.

2. Label the strip "A", "B", "C", and "D" with a few centimeters between each

   letter.

A	B	C	D

3. Place the beans in different directions on the labels with clear tape. They

   should look like the following:

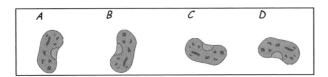

In this experiment the students will investigate the signals of gravitropism and phototropism.

Have the students read the entire experiment before writing the hypothesis. Have them predict whether or not the direction the seed is placed in the jar will affect the growth of the roots and stems. Also have them predict what effect the lack of sunlight will have on those beans placed in the dark.

Example hypotheses:

"Only the bean facing downward (bean D) will grow properly."
"Only beans A and B will grow properly."
"The direction of the bean will not make any difference, and all beans will grow with the roots downward and the stems upward."
"The stems for the beans in the dark will not grow upward."

Any bean type should work for this experiment. Peas will also work, but their orientation may be more difficult to determine.

Two jars will be used. One jar is placed in the dark and the other jar will be kept exposed to sunlight.   The questions that will be addressed are whether or not sunlight is responsible for making the shoots grow up, and whether gravity is enough to cause the roots to grow downward and the shoots to grow upward even without sunlight.

4. Place the paper with the attached beans gently inside the small jar. The beans should be between the jar and the paper.

5. Place one or two more beans in between the paper and the jar, but don't tape these. These beans will be opened and examined before the roots completely emerge.

6. Add some water to the bottom of the jar, but don't submerge the beans.

7. Cover the jar with plastic wrap and secure it with a rubber band. Place the jar in direct sunlight.

8. With the second jar, repeat steps 1-7, but place the jar in a dark room.

9. In a few days the beans will start to grow. When the beans begin to change, take out one of the loose beans and gently cut it open. Try to identify the different parts of the embryo.

10. Continue to observe the growth of the beans. Watch and record their changes every few days. Try to determine if the beans placed in different directions grow differently. Compare the beans grown in the light with those grown in the dark.

Results:

Draw the parts of the embryo here:

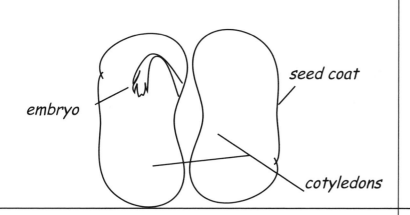

Sometimes, one or more of the beans fail to grow. If a bean fails to grow, it can be replaced with a new bean. Soak a few beans in water overnight and replace the failed bean with the water-soaked bean. Do not soak the beans more than overnight to a few days. If the beans sit in water for too long, they will rot.

In each jar, place only a little bit of water and secure the top with plastic wrap. Allow the paper to contact the water, but do not allow the beans to soak in the water. It may be necessary to add more water to the jars as the experiment proceeds.

Before any visible shoots begin to emerge from the beans, take out one or more of the loose beans and carefully cut them lengthwise. A small embryo should be visible. Have the students draw what they observe. Discuss with them how the fleshy part of the bean provides food for the embryo during the early stages of germination.

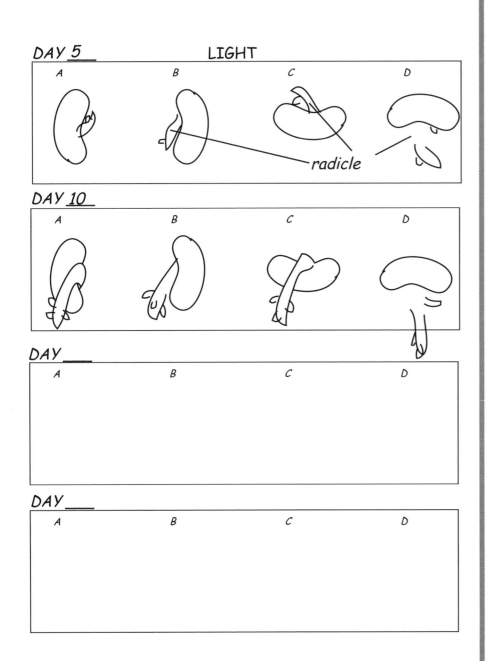

DAY 5   LIGHT

A   B   C   D

radicle

DAY 10

A   B   C   D

DAY ___

A   B   C   D

DAY ___

A   B   C   D

Have the students record the changes in the beans as they grow.   It should take about two weeks for the beans to have good roots and long shoots extending. Make sure to continue the experiment until all of the beans are growing. One or more of the beans can be replaced by the extra beans if they fail to grow.

The radicle should begin to emerge from the bean around Day 5, although this may vary depending on the amount of water and light present. Initially, the roots grow in the direction the bean is placed. Some will grow up, some will grow sideways, and some will grow down. By Day 10, the roots should turn and begin to migrate downward for all of the beans. Compare the beans in the light with those in the dark. The direction of the roots should be independent of the presence of light, and all of the beans should have roots extending downward.

Have the students note any differences among the beans.

record your observations for each bean on the previous pages. It may take several days to see a change. Record the day that you observe a change. Draw a picture of each bean on the days you observe a change.

Conclusions:

_____

_____

_____

_____

_____

_____

_____

_____

_____

_____

_____

_____

_____

_____

_____

_____

Have the students write valid conclusions based on the data they have collected.

Some example are as follows:

"The beans in the dark did not grow differently from the beans in the light."

"The direction the beans were placed did not affect the direction the roots and stems grew."

"None of the beans grew."

It is important that the conclusions the students write be based only on the data collected for this experiment, even if the experiment did not work.

Review

Define the following terms:

seed: *a small plant embryo and supply of food encased in a tough outer shell*

seedling: *the young plant that forms from a seed*

seed coat: *the tough outer shell of a seed*

cotyledon: *the fleshy part of the seed that supplies the embryo with food*

embryo: *the small plant inside a seed*

germination: *the process of a seed beginning to grow and turn into a plant*

Name two plant signals.

1.   *sunlight*

2.   *gravity*

List the four stages in the life cycle of a flowering plant.

1.   *flower to fruit with seeds*

2.   *seeds to germinating plant*

3.   *germinating plant to young seedling*

4.   *young seedling to mature plant*

NOTES:

Chapter 6: Protists I

Time Required:

    Text reading - 1 hour
    Experimental - 1 hour

Experimental setup:

    Order protozoa kit one week prior
    Practice using light microscope

Additional Materials:

    Protozoa

Overall Objectives

The students will be introduced to the microscopic organisms known as protists. They will also be introduced to the function and use of a microscope.

6.1 Introduction

Protists are members of the kingdom Protista.

[NOTE: In some texts, the term protist refers only to the microscopic species. In the 1970's and 80's, the boundaries of the kingdom Protista were expanded to include some multicellular organisms, such as seaweeds and slime molds, and the name of the kingdom was changed to Protoctista. In this chapter we will focus only on the microscopic varieties which will be called protists or protozoa.]

Protists are found everywhere there is water. Protists are found in both salt and fresh water, and in soil. Some well-known protists include the following:

> malarial parasites
> red-tide organisms
> diatoms
> potato-blight organisms
> Giardia
> African sleeping sickness organisms

Protists have been difficult to classify because they are eukaryotes and can have both plant and animal-like qualities. Protist is an "umbrella term" that fits those organisms that can not be easily placed into any other kingdom.

6.2 The microscope

This section introduces the students to the light microscope. There are many different types of microscopes today, including the light microscope, the electron microscope, and the scanning tunneling and scanning force microscopes.

Light microscopes use lenses and light to magnify small objects and make them appear larger. If a light microscope is available, it would be good to discuss the various parts of the microscope at this time.

A sample is placed below the lens, and a light source is placed below the sample. The observer looks through the lens at the sample below. If the lenses are powerful enough, individual cells can be seen. Plant and animal cells are between 10 and 100 microns in size (one micron is 1/1000 of a millimeter). A human hair is about 200 microns in diameter. Bacteria are smaller than plant or animal cells at about 1 micron in diameter. The unaided eye can easily visualize objects as small as 1mm, so a magnification of 10X to 1000X allows us to see animal cells to bacteria.

Robert Hooke is traditionally credited with observing the first cells in 1665. However, Galileo adapted lenses for use in microscopy as early as 1614. Hooke seems to have coined the term "cell," which comes from the Latin word *cella,* meaning *small room* or *cubicle.* It appears that Hooke did not observe living cells. Anton van Leeuwenhoek is credited with the discovery of little animals that he called "aminacules." He observed the organisms we now call protists in pond water.

6.3 Movement

On page 42 of the student text, the three main groupings of protists are presented. These groupings are based primarily on how the organism moves.

The three groupings are ciliates, flagellates, and amoebas.

The ciliates include paramecium and stentor. This group is characterized by many small hair-like projections on their bodies called cilia. The cilia "beat" rhythmically, propelling the organism smoothly through the water. By controlling the beating pattern and speed, ciliates can turn and back up.

The flagellates include the uniflagellar species like euglena and the dinoflagellates (two flagella) like ceratium and pfiesteria. Flagellates move using "whips" that propel them through the water.

Though they have a simple appearance under the microscope, cilia and flagella are actually very sophisticated machines. Each whip contains strands of long aggregate molecules called microtubules. As the microtubules slide past each other, the whip, or cilia, changes orientation. When the microtubules slide in the opposite direction, the whip changes orientation and these successive changes cause the cilia to beat or the flagella to whip.

Amoebas (also called rhizopods) do not have flagella or cilia for swimming, but rather use pseudopodia to move and feed. Pseudopods are "false feet" that allow the organism to creep along surfaces.

Amoebas are found in both freshwater and saltwater environments. Some amoebas are harmful to humans, such as Entamoeba histolytica, which causes amoebic dysentery.

6.4 Summary

Discuss the main points of this chapter with the students.

Ask the students to think about the plant and animal qualities protists have. Ask them how protists eat and move and which of those things are like plants or animals. For example,

Some protists use the sun's energy to make food, just like plants.

Some protists eat other protists, just as animals sometimes eat other animals.

Amoebas use "false feet" to move and crawl like animals.

Ask how a microscope makes things look bigger and how, without a microscope, things that are too small for our eyes cannot be seen. Ask the students to think about how exciting it must have been for the first microscopists to discover this new world of tiny organisms.

Discuss with the students the different types of movement protists display and how they are classified by this movement.

Experiment 6:   How do they move?   Date: _____

Objective: *In this experiment, three types of protozoa will be observed. Based on their movement, protozoa in pond water will be characterized.*

Hypothesis: *We can tell the difference between ciliates and flagellates in pond water.*

Materials:

  microscope with a 10X objective
  concavity culture slides (WARD'S Glass Depression Slides, 14-D-3510)
  3 eye droppers
  fresh pond water or water mixed with soil
  Protozoa (Basic) study kit (WARD'S Protist Set 1, 87-D-1530)

Experiment:

1. Familiarize yourself with your microscope before beginning this lesson. Read the instruction manual for your microscope, if it is available, and try to look at any prepared samples that may have come with your microscope. If you already know how to operate a microscope, skip this step.
2. Take one of the protozoa samples and place a small droplet onto a glass slide that has been correctly positioned in the microscope.
3. Observe the movement of the protozoa. If the organisms move too quickly, apply a droplet of Protoslo to the glass slide.
4. Patiently observe the movement of the protozoa. Note the type of protozoa in the Results section. Try to describe how the protozoa moves. Write down as many observations as you can.
5. Repeat step 4 with the other two protozoan types.

NOTE: This is an optional experiment. If a microscope is unavailable, or if protozoa cannot be ordered, this experiment can be skipped.

In this experiment the students will examine the three different types of protozoa discussed in this chapter and individual protozoa in pond water to identify based on movement.

Have the students read the experiment before writing a hypothesis.

Microscope recommendation:

Gravitas Publications [www.gravitaspublications.com] sells a "student" microscope for $14.95. It is made of plastic and is very durable. It has exceptional clarity for viewing protozoa and is easy for students to use. Together with the plastic well slides this small microscope works very well.

The difficulty with this experiment is viewing the tiny organisms through the tiny eyepiece of a microscope. It is sometimes difficult for younger students to align their eye directly into the lens so that the sample is visible. Also, these organisms often swim rapidly through the field of view, and it is easy to get frustrated trying to observe them. Patience with this experiment is a must. It may be useful for the students to spend one day "playing" with the microscope and observing prepared slides, or pieces of hair, or other small objects before attempting to view the protozoa.

6. Now take a droplet of fresh pond water and place it on a slide to view under the microscope. Try to determine the types of protozoa you observe based on how the organism moves. Write your results in the Results section.

Results:

Name _____

Describe movement:_____

Name _____

Describe movement:_____

Name _____

Describe movement:_____

Have the students draw the protozoa and describe their movement in the boxes.

The euglena will tend to move in a single direction or not move at all, but "hover" just under the light.

The paramecium will move all over the place. It will roll, move forward and backward, and spin. There are usually other things in the water with the paramecium. Have the students note what happens when a paramecium "bumps" into other objects or other paramecia.

The amoeba move very slowly. It can be difficult to obseve the amoeba. The amoeba are usually on the bottom of the container. Allow the container to sit for 30 minutes and then remove the solution at the very bottom to place in the slide. The amoeba should be visible, but they are clear. Prestained live amoeba can be purchased from WARD's Natural Science if it proves too frustrating to view these organisms (95-D-0224).

Draw what you observe in the pond water.

Have the students observe the organisms in pond water with their microscope. Have them draw as many organisms as they can find.

See if they can identify any protists by observing their movement and comparing this movement to the known protists they observed earlier.

Conclusions:

We did not see any protozoa, only dirt.

We observed small protozoa that swam like paramecia.

We observed some amoeba.

We saw some organisms that we could not identify, but that looked liked protozoa.

Have the students write conclusions based on their observations. The conclusions will vary depending on whether the experiment worked. It is important that the students write conclusions based on their observations. Some examples are given.

Review

Define the following terms:

protist   *A small eukaryotic creature that can be like both an animal and like a plant.*

microscope   *An instrument used to look at small objects.*

cilia   *Small "hairs" found on certain protists that help them move.*

flagellum   *A long whip attached at one end to many types of protists that enable the protists to move.*

pseudopod   *"False feet" found on an amoeba that allow it to move and eat.*

Draw a paramecium.

Draw a Euglena.

Draw an amoeba.

How do euglena and paramecia move?   *Euglena and paramecia move rapidly with small hairs and whips.*

How does an amoeba move?   *An amoeba moves slowly with pseudopods.*

NOTES

Chapter 7: Protists II

Time Required:

> Text reading - 1 hour
> Experimental - 1 hour

Experimental setup:

> Use protozoa kit from Chapter 6
> Make Congo-Red stained yeast

Additional Materials:

> Protozoa kit from Chapter 6
> Congo Red stain (WARD'S Natural
> Science 944 V 9504)

Overall Objectives

In this chapter the students will be introduced to the feeding mechanisms of several protozoa. They will see how protists can have both plant-like and animal-like characteristics. They will observe the feeding habits of certain protozoa.

7.1 Nutrition

Discuss with the students how they get their nutrition. Review Chapter 8 of Chemistry Level I and discuss energy molecules. Also, discuss how they are not like plants which can use the sun to make food.

Ask them how they think small animals like protozoa get their food.

7.2 How euglena eat

Euglena are photosynthetic protists. They have chloroplasts, just like plants, and use the sun's energy to make food through photosynthesis. Another photosynthetic protist is the Volvox, which is a protist that lives in large groups or colonies.

Euglena must be able to "detect" sunlight in order to survive. This is accomplished with a small spot near the flagellum called the eyespot or stigma. The stigma is actually a collection of photosensitive pigments that absorb photons of light. The stigma can collect light in only one direction and thus serves as a light signal to the euglena. The euglena is able to orient itself in the water so that it is exposed to sufficient light for photosynthesis.

7.3 How paramecia eat

Paramecia are not photosynthetic and therefore rely on outside food sources for survival.

Paramecia have a specialized feeding structure called the oral groove. The oral groove leads to the cell mouth or cytostome. The oral groove has cilia surrounding the entrance. The cilia beat in a circular fashion and sweep the food into the oral groove.

Once inside, the food travels to the cytostome [cellular mouth] and into the food vacuole. The food vacuole is a little sack which contains digestive enzymes. This digestive mechanism is called intracellular digestion. The food vacuole travels throughout the cell, digesting the food as it goes. The waste is excreted through a small pore called a cytoproct (cellular anus).

7.4 How amoebas eat

Amoebas eat by an entirely different mechanism than either euglena or paramecia. Amoeba engulf their food using pseudopods. This process is called "phagocytosis." The amoeba moves the pseudopods in the direction of the prey, eventually engulfing it. A food vacuole is formed around the caught prey and the membranes fuse with lysosomes which inject digestive enzymes. There is no cytoproct in an amoeba, and wastes are eliminated thorough the membrane.

7.5 How other protozoa eat

Page 49 of the student text shows different protozoa exhibit other eating mechanisms. The illustrations show two protists that use different methods to capture prey. The didinium uses a long tentacle to capture food and the podophyra uses its tentacles to attach and remove the contents of its prey.

7.6 Summary

Discuss with the students the main points of this chapter. Explain that protozoa have both plant-like and animal-like qualities. Explain that protozoa are uniquely designed and are amazing little single-celled creatures.

NOTES

Experiment 7:   How do they eat?   Date: _____

Objective: *In this experiment, both paramecia and amoeba will be observed*
              while eating yeast.

Hypothesis: _____
              _____

Materials:
          Protozoa study kit [same as in Experiment 6]
          Congo Red stain (WARD'S Natrual Science, 944 V 9504)
          Baker's yeast
          Distilled water
          Microscope
          Microscope slides
          Eye droppers (3)

Making Congo-Red-stained yeast:

     This step needs to be completed before continuing with the experiment.
       • Add one teaspoon of dried yeast to ½ cup of distilled water. Allow
         it to dissolve.
       • Add one droplet of Congo Red dye to one droplet of yeast mixture.
         Observe the mixture under the microscope. You should be able to
         observe the individual yeast cells stained red.

Experiment:

1. Take either the paramecia or amoeba samples and place a small droplet onto a
   glass slide that has been correctly positioned in the microscope.

2. Take a small droplet of the Congo Red stained yeast and place it into the droplet of protozoa.

3. Patiently observe the protozoa and note the red colored yeast. Try to
   describe how the protozoa eats. Write down as many observations as you can.

NOTE: This is an optional experiment. If a microscope is unavailable, or if protozoa cannot be ordered, this experiment can be skipped.

In this experiment the students will examine how two different protozoa eat. Yeast will be used as food.

Have the students read the entire experiment before writing the hypothesis. Have them predict whether or not the protozoa will eat the yeast and how each protist will eat.

The Congo Red stained yeast will be ingested by the protozoa. It may take time for this observation. Once ingested, the red stained yeast will turn blue.

4. Repeat steps 2-4 with the other protozoa.

5. Record your observations below.

Results:

Draw a picture showing how amoebas eat

Have the students draw their observations in the box.

Have the students draw their observations in the box.

Draw a picture showing how paramecia eat.

onclusions:

_____
_____
_____
_____
_____
_____
_____
_____
_____
_____
_____
_____
_____
_____
_____
_____

Have the students write conclusions based on their observations. If the experiment did not work, this should be written as a conclusion.

Review

Define the following terms:

stigma — *Also called the eyespot, it detects light for the euglena.*

food vacuole — *The sack inside a paramecium or amoeba that holds and digests food.*

phagocytosis — *A process by which a protist engulfs and eats its food.*

oral groove — *The opening in paramecia that takes in food.*

cytoplasm — *The inside material of a cell.*

What is *didinium*? — *A protozoa that eats paramecium whole.*

What is *podophyra*? — *A protozoa that eats paramecium using tentacles and eats the insides.*

Chapter 8:   The Frog Life Cycle

Time Required:

   Text reading - 1 hour
   Experimental - about 4 weeks

Experimental setup:

   Purchase tadpole kit or collect
   tadpoles from a pond

Additional Materials:

   Live tadpoles
   Small aquarium
   Tadpole food
   medium-sized rocks

Overall Objectives

In this chapter the students will be introduced to the life cycle of frogs. They will examine the various stages of the life cycle and observe a tadpole changing into an adult frog.

8.1 Introduction

Frogs are amphibians and are in the class Amphibia. The term "amphibia" means "both lives" and refers to those creatures that live in both water and on land for at least part of their life. Not all amphibians live their lives both in the water and on land. Some amphibians spend their whole lives on land or in the water. However, even those that live almost exclusively on land need to be near water in a moist environment.

Frogs are not the only amphibians. The class Amphibia also includes salamanders, newts, mud puppies, sirens, and caecilians. There are about 5,000 known species of amphibians. Frogs are in the order Anura, which means "without tail," since frogs lose their tails as adults. Salamanders do not lose their tails and are in the order Caudata, which means "tail to bear." If you live near a lake or pond where salamanders live take your students on a field trip to find salamanders or other amphibians that may be common in your area.

8.2 Stage I: The egg

All amphibians begin life as an egg. The amount of time spent as an egg varies from a few hours to a few weeks. The outside of the egg is not made of a tough outer shell, like a chicken egg, but instead, has a jelly-like coating covering the outside. Often the eggs are laid in clumps or in long strings. The jelly-like coating protects the eggs from drying out and helps them stick together.

The maternal parent will often attend the eggs until the time they hatch. Some frogs, such as the Pipa, carry the eggs and young on their backs; and the Rheobatrachus develop and carry their young in their mouth!

8.3 Stage II: The tadpole

When the eggs hatch, tadpoles or pollywogs emerge. The tadpole stage is the larval stage since the tadpoles are immature amphibians. Tadpoles differ from their adult counterparts in significant ways. They have tails and gills, but no eyelids.

The size of a tadpole varies depending on the species. Often, tadpoles are larger than the adult. In general, tadpole size increases with length of the developmental period: smaller tadpoles for shorter developmental stages and larger tadpoles for longer developmental stages. The Harlequin tadpole grows up to 10 inches and takes four months to develop. However, the adult frog is only 3 inches long. This reduction in size is called "shrinkage."

8.4 Stage III: From tadpole to frog

The process of changing from a juvenile tadpole into an adult frog is called metamorphosis. The many changes that occur in frogs during metamorphosis include the emergence of limbs and the absorption of the tail into the body. The skin thickens, and lungs develop as the external gills disappear. There are also dramatic changes that occur in the digestive track associated with a change in diet.

ther amphibians, such as salamanders, do not undergo such dramatic changes as frogs do.

5 Stage IV: The adult frog

here are many different species of frogs, and they make up the biggest rder of amphibians. There are true frogs, tree frogs, tropical frogs, ads, narrow-mouth toads, and spade-foot toads. All of these species ffer slightly in their color and characteristics, but they do have some milar features.

ost species of frogs have well-developed hearing and have a embrane located just behind the eyes. This membrane is called the mpanic membrane or tympanum. This membrane vibrates in response sound.

ost frogs have eyes that see very well. Land frogs have an eyelid, and ater frogs have a thin membrane covering the eye for protection. Eye olor and shape varies, and most frogs have horizontal pupils.

rogs come in a variety of colors. Many poisonous frogs are brightly olored, such as the Dendrobatids. (Also known as poison dart frogs.) heir bright colors warn potential predators that they are poisonous. any local zoos have exhibits showing a variety of poisonous frogs.

6 Summary

eview the summary statements at the end of the chapter.

NOTES

Experiment 8:   From Tadpole to Frog   Date: ——————————

Objective: *We will observe the change (metamorphosis) as a tadpole turns into a frog*

Materials:

    tadpole
    tadpole food
    small aquarium
    distilled water

Experiment:

1. Fill the aquarium $\frac{1}{2}$ to $\frac{3}{4}$ full with distilled water.

2. Add the live tadpoles.

3. Feed the tadpoles according to the directions.

4. Observe the changes the tadpole makes over the course of 4 to 6 weeks.

5. Record your observations in the Results section. See if you can identify the different stages of the tadpole outlined in this chapter (note when the legs emerge, note the time it takes for the front legs to emerge etc.)

In this experiment, the students will observe the life cycle of a frog.

If possible, observe the growth and development of a frog from a local pond or stream. If this is not possible, tadpoles and/or frog eggs can be purchased. Most purchased frogs cannot be released into the wild. Check with the supply company to find out what to do with your adult frogs.

Resources:

A tadpole kit can be ordered from Grow-A-Frog. This tadpole is transparent so the internal organs can be easily visualized. There is some difficulty in keeping the adult frogs alive once the tails are completely gone, but the tadpoles did live to the adult stage.

    Grow-A-Frog Kit
    Three Rivers of Brooksville, Inc.
    P.O. Box 10369
    Brooksville, Florida 34603

WARD'S. also sells frogs, tadpoles and frog eggs.

    Frog eggs: 87 V 8205
    Frogs living specimen : 87 V 8195
    Early tadpoles: 87 V 8210

    NOTE: *Xenopus* is not recommened.

Draw the various stages in the life cycle of frogs.

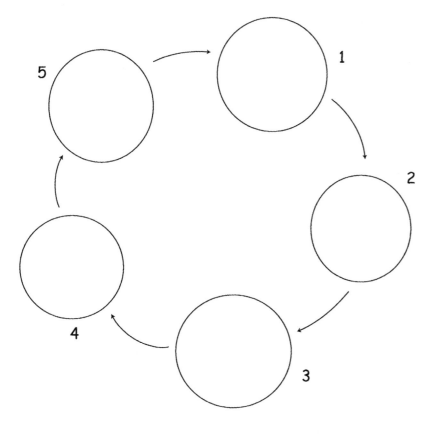

Draw the various stages in the life cycle of frogs.

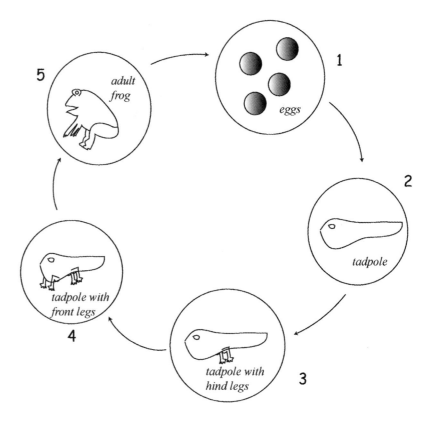

Label the parts of the frog.

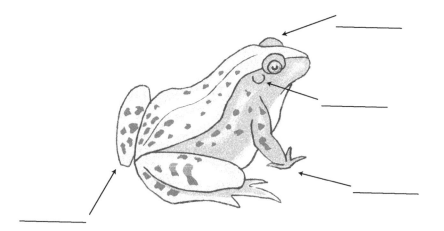

Label the parts of the frog.

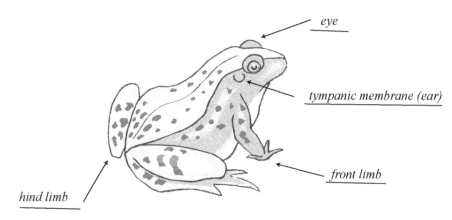

eye

tympanic membrane (ear)

front limb

hind limb

Results:

Week

1 _____

2 _____

3 _____

4 _____

5 _____

6 _____

7 _____

8 _____

9 _____

10 _____

11 _____

12 _____

Have the students record the changes they observe over the course of several weeks.

Have them note in particular if the hind legs emerge before the front legs. Also have them observe whether the hind legs begin as buds and whether the front legs come out fully developed.

Conclusions:

_____

_____

_____

_____

_____

Have the students write some conclusions based on their observations.

Review

Define the following terms:

spawning   *An event where an adult female frog lays eggs to be fertilized by the male frog.*

amphibian   *A term that means "both lives;" an animal that lives both on land and in water.*

metamorphosis   *A term that refers to the change from tadpole to adult in the case of frogs.*

tympanic membrane   *The ear of a frog.*

NOTES

Chapter 9 : The Butterfly Life Cycle

Time Required:

    Text reading - 20 minutes
    Experimental - about 4 weeks

Experimental setup:

    Purchase butterfly kit one week prior

Additional Materials:

    WARD'S Natural Sciences
    (www.wardsci.com)

    Insect Lore
    Butterfly Garden (221)
    (www.insectlore.com)

Overall Objectives

In this chapter the students will examine the life cycle of the butterfly. The students will study a different kind of metamorphosis from the class Insecta.

9.1 Introduction

Butterflies, moths, and skippers are in the order Lepidoptera. This name reflects the fact that these insects have "scaly wings." There are more than 100,000 known species, and it is the second largest insect order next to the beetles, order Coleoptera. Moths are the most abundant species in this order, but butterflies are the most brightly colored and often the most familiar species.

Moths and butterflies come in a variety of shapes, sizes, and coloration. The smallest moths and butterflies have wing spans not much larger than the size of a pencil eraser. The wingspan of the largest butterflies can extend almost one foot.

The life cycle of Lepidoptera consists of four stages; egg, larva, pupa, and adult. Some species develop as fast as three weeks. Other species can take up to three years to fully develop.

Moths and butterflies are found on every continent except Antarctica. Many species migrate from one place to another, but only the Monarch butterfly makes true two-way migration from Mexico to North America and then back again.

9.2 Stage I: the egg

The first stage in the life cycle of butterflies is the egg. The number of eggs laid can vary from a few hundred to several thousand. Eggs are deposited onto suitable food sources such as leaves or branches.

Butterfly eggs come in a variety of shapes and sizes. The outer coating can be smooth and shiny, like Monarch eggs, or decorated with elaborate grooves and depressions. Some eggs are deposited as single eggs, and others are deposited in groups.

The hatching of eggs coincides with favorable weather and growth of the food source. The eggs can exchange oxygen with the air via small passages in the shell, whether wet or dry.

When the egg is hatched, the larvae, or caterpillar, eats the food source. Many species of moth and butterfly are limited to only a small group of suitable plants. Many species, therefore, remain in only one habitat. Species that can eat more variety are found in many different habitats.

9.3 Stage II: the caterpillar

Once the egg hatches, a larvae, or caterpillar emerges. The caterpillar's sole function is to eat! This stage in the life cycle of many butterflies is the chief nutritional stage, and a caterpillar consumes many times its weight in food during this part of the cycle.

Caterpillars can be brightly colored, hairy, or plain in color, depending on the species. Those caterpillars that live and feed covered by foliage or in burrows, are mostly plain in color. Caterpillars that feed in the open are usually brightly colored with ornamentation such as hair or horns which help defend against predators.

The larval stage of butterflies can last anywhere from a few weeks to several years, depending on the species. During this time, the caterpillar grows and molts, shedding its old skin as many as four or five times.

Once the caterpillar has completed the larval development stage, it stops eating and finds a suitable place to weave a cocoon. Here the pupal stage begins.

9.4 Stage III: the cocoon

The third stage in the butterfly life cycle is the pupal stage. The caterpillar has completed the growth and development of the larval stage and is ready for hibernation and metamorphosis.

Many species spin cocoons on the underside of branches or other surfaces. A small bit of silk is woven at one end, and the caterpillar tests the strength of this "button" to ensure it will hold. The caterpillar then spins the silk around itself making a tough cocoon. Many cocoons are made of silk alone, but some species incorporate leaves, hair, or chewed wood pulp. The cocoon sometimes has a seam that helps the adult butterfly emerge.

The pupal stage varies depending on the species. Many small species take only a few days to a few weeks to develop. Other larger species may take several months. The adult will emerge only when conditions are right. Some cocoons have been known to survive several years before the adult finally comes out.

9.5 Stage IV: the butterfly

The final stage in the butterfly life cycle is the adult stage. Once the cocoon has completed the time required for metamorphosis, and when the conditions permit, the adult butterfly will emerge from the cocoon.

The adult is fully formed inside the cocoon. To exit the cocoon, the butterfly wriggles until it is finally free. Some species have spines along their back to help bore holes in the cocoon and push out the walls.

When the young butterfly emerges, it cannot fly yet. The wings are wrinkled up, and the butterfly must pump fluid into them. Often the butterfly crawls to a place where it can hang with its head up allowing the fluid to flow into the wings. It may take several minutes or even a few hours before the wings are stiff enough for flight.

The main purpose of the adult stage in the life cycle of butterflies and moths is reproduction. Nutrition is essential only in a few species during this stage. Food is taken in only for supplying energy for flight. Many butterflies and moths travel great distances during the adult stage. In North America many moths migrate to Canada, and, in Europe, many butterflies and moths migrate to Scandinavia. Once a butterfly has found a mate, the female lays eggs and the cycle repeats.

9.6 Summary

Discuss the summary statements for this chapter.

Experiment 9 : From caterpillar to butterfly   Date: _____

Objective: *We will observe the change (metamorphosis) as a caterpillar turns into a butterfly.*

Hypotheis: _____

Materials:

    caterpillar or butterfly kit
    small cage

Experiment:

1. Follow the directions on the butterfly kit for proper care of your caterpillar or provide food for your local caterpillar from the leaves on which it was found.

2. Fill out the life cycle chart on page 47.

3. Over the course of the next several weeks, observe any changes your caterpillar undergoes.

4. Record how much food your caterpillar eats.

5 Record how many times the caterpillar molts.

6. Record where the caterpillar spins its cocoon.

7. If you can observe the caterpillar emerging, record how long before it can fly.

In this experiment, the students will observe the change from caterpillar to butterfly.

If possible have the students collect local caterpillars and house them in a small cage. If a caterpillar can be located, take several leaves from the plant where it was found for food. If a local caterpillar cannot be found, caterpillar kits can be purchased.

Resources:

WARD'S Natural Sciences sells several different butterly pupae; www. wardsci.com

Also Insect Lore sells several butterfly kits. Insect Lore has excellent customer service, nearly 100% survival rate with a good guarantee on their product, and they allow you to designate a week in which you receive your specimen.

Draw the various stages in the life cycle of a butterfly,

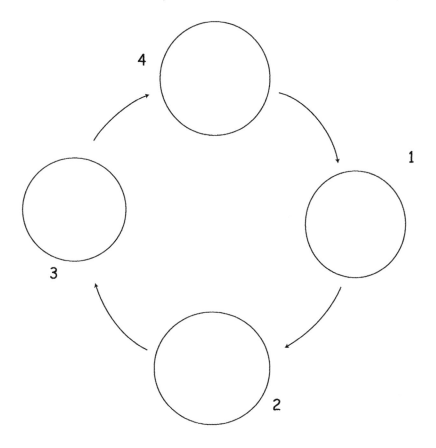

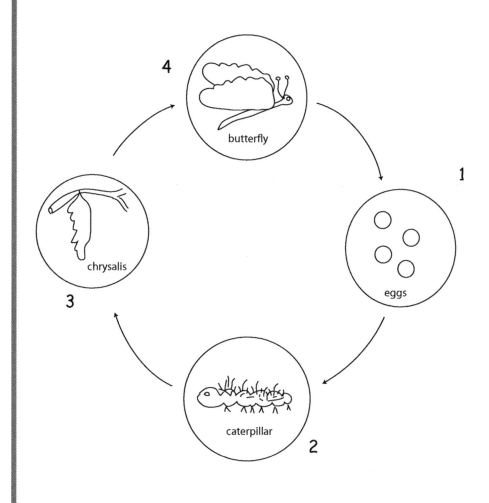

Results:

Week	Amount of food eaten	Molting?	Other observations
1			
2			
3			
4			
5			
6			
7			
8			
9			
10			
11			
12			

Conclusions:

_____

_____

_____

_____

_____

_____

Have the students write their observations in the Results section. It may not be possible to determine how much the caterpillar eats or see all of the molting stages. Have the students record any other observations such as movement or periods of inactivity.

Have the students write some conclusions based on their observations. Some possibilities are the following:

"I observed the caterpillar eating only three full leaves."
"I recorded only three molts for the caterpillar."
"It took two weeks for the caterpillar to form a cocoon."

Again, help the students be accurate with their concluding statements.

Review

Define the following terms:

Lepidoptera — *Term meaning "wings with scales;" the order of insects that includes butterflies, skippers, and moths.*

larval stage — *The caterpillar stage of the butterfly life cycle.*

molting — *The process of shedding skin that occurs when a caterpillar or other animal grows.*

pupal stage — *The chrysalis stage of the butterfly life cycle.*

chrysalis — *The pupa of a butterfly.*

imago — *The adult stage of an insect.*

NOTES

_____

_____

_____

_____

_____

_____

_____

_____

_____

_____

_____

_____

_____

_____

_____

_____

_____

_____

_____

_____

_____

_____

Chapter 10 : Our Balanced World

Time Required:

    Text reading - 20 minutes
    Experimental - about 3-5 weeks

Experimental setup:

    NONE

Additional Materials:

    See materials list page 168.

Overall Objectives

In this chapter the students will be introduced to the concept of an ecosystem and the often delicate balance that exists within an ecosystem.

10.1 Introduction

The earth can be considered a global ecosystem, that is, an ecosystem that constitutes the entire globe. Within the global ecosystem, smaller ecosystems are found. These include anything from a small pond to large lakes, oceans, and other habitats.

10.2 Ecosystems

Discuss with the students the balance observed between plants, animals, and other organisms on the planet. Have the students think about the plants and animals they know, or have found in their backyard or local environment. Ask the students what is required for plants and animals to live. Lead a discussion using the following questions:

1. What do plants need to live? (with sunlight, water, air, nutrients) Where do plants get their food? (photosynthesis, soil, air) What do they need for food? (carbon dioxide, water, nitrogen, other minerals)
2. What do animals need to live? (food, air, water) Where do animals get their food? (plants, other animals)
3. What do we need to live? (food, water, air, shelter, clothing). Where do we get our food? (plants, animals) Where do we get our shelter and clothing? (plants, animals, non-living things like rocks)
4. What would happen to the plants if there was no water?
5. What would happen to the animals if there were no plants?
6. What would happen to us if there were no plants or animals?

Discuss with the students the meaning of a *cycle*. Ask them if they have observed other cycles. They should reply that the life cycles of a frog and a butterfly are types of cycles. A cycle is simply a sequence of events that repeats itself.

Discuss with the students the difference between the cycle of a living creature and the cycles involved in non living phenomena, such as water. The life cycle of a living creature depends on the survival of the creature. Once the animal or plant is extinct, or no longer surviving, the cycle ceases. The cycle of the materials a living thing is made of continues on even if the creature dies. The water cycle, on the other hand, continues. The water levels may vary and the cycle may change patterns, but it continues unless the earth itself disappears.

10.3 The food cycle

Discuss the food cycle of living things. All living things require some energy source for survival. The food cycles of living things are coupled. Microorganisms use the remains of decaying animals for food. These microorganisms provide nutrients for plants. Plants are the primary food source of many animals. Other animals feed directly off of animals and do not eat plants.

Show the students the connection between the various animals and their food sources. Explain how each one is dependent on the other for survival.

10.4 The air cycle

Discuss with the students how we get our air to breathe. Explain that air is also part of a cycle. We inhale oxygen and exhale carbon dioxide. Explain that carbon dioxide is a gas, just like oxygen. Conveniently, plants use carbon dioxide to make food for photosynthesis, and they give off oxygen. This is pretty handy. Ask the studetns what would happen if animals used carbon dioxide and gave off oxygen like plants (where would we get more carbon dioxide?)

Discuss with the students how the balance of oxygen and carbon dioxide helps keep everything working.

10.5 The water cycle

Discuss with the students how water is cycled from place to place. The oceans provide clouds with abundant rain water. When the clouds travel over land, they deposit their water in the form of rain. The rain collects in rivers, streams, and underground aquifers, providing water for many living things. Small streams feed larger streams which feed rivers. Rivers empty their water back into the ocean, and the cycle repeats.

Water is vital for living creatures. Some living things can go without water for many days, even weeks, but no living thing can survive without some water.

The weather cycles are driven by solar radiation and by the spinning of the earth on its axis among other things. This is conveniently balanced to provide the variety of winds, rain, snow, and hot weather for the globe. The atmosphere also insulates the earth, providing the temperatures needed for life. The atmosphere, although transparent, traps heat close to the earth's surface, keeping a moderately warm average temperature.

There are other examples of cycles that provide balance to our ecosystem. Nitrogen, phosphorus, sulfur, and carbon are all cycled throughout the globe.

10.6 Summary

Discuss with the students how all of these cycles are coupled to each other. The clouds provide water for the plants. The plants provide oxygen and food for the animals. The animals provide food for other animals and small organisms.

Experiment 10: Making an ecosystem   Date: _____

Objective: _In this experiment, we will try to build an ecosystem and observe_

_what happens over the course of several weeks._____

Materials:

    clear tank with a solid lid

    small plants

    soil

    small bugs such as worms, ants, small beetles, etc.

Experiment:

1. Take the glass or plastic container and cover the bottom with water.

2. Place the lid on the container and allow it to sit overnight.

3. Record your observations in Part I A of the Results section.

4. Remove the lid and let it sit overnight again.

5. Record your results in Part I B of the Results section.

6. Place the soil on the bottom of the container. Put in enough soil to fill

   the container about 1/3 full.

7. Plant the small plants in the soil.

8. Add the small bugs to the plants.

9. Place the lid on the container and in Part II record any changes in your

   ecosystem over the next several weeks.

In this experiment the students will build a small ecosystem.

In the first part of the experiment students will observe the evaporation and condensation of water.   In Part I A the water will not escape the container, but instead condense on the top or sides. The condensed water will "rain" back to the bottom. Explain that this is how water cycles in our atmosphere. In Part I B, the lid is left off. Explain how in this case, the water disappears altogether and is not cycled back to the system. Explain that if we did not have an atmosphere, the water on our planet would disappear.

Closed ecosystems are difficult to maintain.   The food sources, light, and mineral nutrients need to be properly balanced.

It is recommended that a closed ecosystem be attempted so that the students can observe the changes and problems that occur. For this ecosystem use a few plants and some small animals like bugs and worms. These living things may die, but it is possible the closed system may work long enough to observe the interactions of the various organisms.

To make a closed ecosystem, pick only one or two plants and a few small bugs. It is not necessary to have many plants and animals which it will only complicate the experiment. Don't use frogs, lizards or other larger animals. Anticipate the food sources for the plants and animals you choose. Add some enriched soil. This can be purchased or can be soil formed with compost. This soil contains the necessary microbes for the ecosystem. Assemble the plants, bugs, and soil and add a little water. Don't add too much water. Seal the box, and the closed ecosystem is complete. Place the ecosystem in indirect sunlight.

Results:

Part I A
_____

Part I B
_____

Part II

Have the students record their observations. For Part I A and B, have them write down what happens to the water.

For Part II students observations can be written or sketched. The observations will vary depending on what happens to the ecosystem. If too much water is added, the plants may begin to mold or die. If there is not enough food for the worms or bugs, they may die. The leaves of the plants may change color if there is not enough nitrogen or other mineral nutrients in the soil.

Conclusions:

_____

_____

_____

_____

_____

_____

_____

_____

_____

_____

_____

Have the students write conclusions based on their observations. If the ecosystem developed problems, have the students try to guess the causes: too much water, too much light, too little light, not enough food, etc.

Discuss with the students how difficult it is to maintain a balanced ecosystem and how remarkable our earth ecosystem is. All of the living and nonliving systems cycle and are balanced in just the right amounts to provide a continuous environment for future generations of living things. Discuss how the orbital path of the earth is elliptical, providing the necessary seasons and how the spinning of the earth causes wind and other necessary weather. Discuss how the sun is placed just far enough not to be too hot, but yet close enough to provide adequate heat and light. All of these factors contribute to making our unique world.

Closed ecosystems can also be purchased. NASA has developed a completely enclosed ecosystem in various sized glass spheres. The system can be purchased from several nature stores (called the Ecosphere). These usually have a few small snails, some shrimp, and aquatic plants. They are completely enclosed and can survive for many years.

Open ecosystems, or terraria can also be made. A terrarium can be easily assembled and can include frogs, lizards, or salamanders. Fish tanks are another kind of open ecosystem. The plants and animals in terraria need an outside source of food and water, and the tanks need to be cleaned, but they have a higher rate of survival.

Review

Define the following terms:

ecosystem   *A community of plants, animals, and other creatures living together.*

cycle   *A series of steps that repeats continuously.*

food cycle   *A cycle with the following steps: plants feed animals, animals feed other animals, animals die and feed microorganisms, microorganisms feed plants.*

air cycle   *A cycle in which animals breathe oxygen and exhale carbon dioxide, plants take in carbon dioxide and give off oxygen.*

water cycle *A cycle in which rain falls on land, feeding rivers and streams; streams feed oceans; ocean water evaporates to supply rain to clouds.*

NOTES

PHYSICS

Materials at a glance

Experiment 1	Experiment 2	Experiment 3	Experiment 4	Experiment 5	Experiment 6	Experiment 7	Experiment 8	Experiment 9	Experiment 10
tennis ball yarn or string (10ft) paper clip marble	slinky paper clips apple lemon or lime banana ruler balance or food scale	stiff cardboard wooden board or plank (3 feet) straight pin or tack scale or balance small to medium-sized toy car banana slices (10-20) pennies	small glass marbles of different size cardboard tube scissors black marking pen ruler two stop watches letter scale or balance	(10-20) copper pennies paper towels aluminum foil salt water voltmeter plastic-coated copper wire, 4"-6" long duct tape (or other strong tape)	small glass jar aluminum foil paper clip duct tape (or other strong tape) plastic or rubber rod balloon silk fabric (2) small magnets iron filings	insulated electrical wire 12 V battery insulating material; foam, plastic, cloth small light bulb electrical tape several small resistors	metal rod electrical wire (10-20) paper clips 12 V battery electrical tape	two prisms flashlight metal can open at both ends aluminum foil rubber band laser pointer long wooden craft stick colored pencils duct tape (or other strong tape)	student selected materials

Chapter 1: What is Physics?

Time Required:

    Text reading - 30 minutes
    Experimental - 1 hour

Experimental setup:

    NONE

Additional Materials:

    NONE

Overall Objectives:

This chapter will introduce the students to a fundamental concept in physics called "physical laws." The students will also examine the scientific method.

1.1 Introduction

This section introduces observations about the physical world. Ask the students to describe several observations they may have noticed.

For example,

What happens when they put on the brakes while riding a bicycle? Do the tires stop immediately? Do they skid?

What happens when they throw a ball into the air? Does it reach the clouds? Does it come down in the same spot?

What happens when they turn on a flashlight? How far can they see the light? Can they see the light of a flashlight in the daytime?

Try to get the students to discuss as many observations as they can. There are no "wrong" answers, and, at this point, the reasons why something happens are not important.

1.2 The basic laws of physics

Ask the students what a "law" is. Think about the law against driving too fast or a law against stealing. Ask them if these laws are ever broken, and if so, why they get broken.

Ask the students some questions about what they have consistently observed. For example,

Have they ever thrown a ball that not come down (except when it ge stuck in a tree)?

Does ice always float?

Does the sun always come up in the morning?

Explain to the students that a law in physics differs from the kinds laws that govern our country. In physics, a law is an overall principle relationship that remains the same and is not broken.

1.3 How do we get laws?

Discuss with the students how we make laws for our country, city, or stat Discuss with them how making city, state, or federal laws involves a lon process where several people decide what kinds of laws to make. Explai that, because there are different people making the laws, some laws ar different from city to city or state to state. For example, the speed lim is different in different states because not everyone in every state agree on what the speed limit should be, the population varies, and there ma be different types of terrain. Explain to the students that government laws are laws we make ourselves and, because of this, the law sometime differs.

Ask the students if they think physical laws are laws we make ourselve Do physical laws differ from state to state? Do they think that a baseba hit from a ballpark in Alaska or Hawaii might be able to reach the clouds Will ice float in Arizona, but sink in New Jersey? The answer is "no," ball will not reach the clouds in Alaska and "yes," ice still floats in Ne Jersey.

xplain to the students that physical laws are not laws we make up urselves. They are regularities in the way things behave that scientists ave discovered. Explain that the physical world is ordered, reliable and onsistent. This orderliness means there are underlying physical laws, or eneral principles, that we can discover to better understand the world.

xplain to the students that physical laws are described by mathematics. ecause the universe is ordered, mathematics can be used to describe recisely the laws that govern it.

4 The scientific method

lthough scientific investigation began with Aristotle, the foundations for e scientific method were not established until the 13th century with Roger acon and further elucidated in the 17th century by René Descartes.

he scientific method has the following five steps:

1) observation
2) formulating a hypothesis
3) experimentation
4) collecting results
5) drawing conclusions

he first step in the scientific method is observation. Discuss with the udents how observations are made. Give some examples of observations ade using sight, hearing, taste, smell, or touch. For example,

Salt is poured on icy roads when it snows.
Lemons are sour. Oranges are sweet.
The sky is blue.

Ice cubes float in soda, water, and milk.
Thunder claps are louder when lightning is close.
Steel balls or marbles are sometimes cold, but cotton balls are not.

Have the students turn these observations into questions as follows:

Why is salt poured on icy roads when it snows?
Why are lemons sour but oranges sweet?
Why is the sky blue?
Why do ice cubes float in soda, water, and milk?
Do ice cubes float in oil?
Why is thunder loudest when lightning is closest?
Why are steel balls or marbles sometimes cold, but cotton balls are not?

Explain to the students that, after making observations and asking questions about these observations, the next step in the scientific method is formulating a hypothesis. Hypotheses are guesses. That is, from an observation and the questions about observations, a statement can be made about why something is a certain way. Although a scientist should attempt to make a good guess, hypotheses do not have to be correct. For example,

1) Salt is put on roads to make rubber tires sticky. (Salt is actually used to lower the freezing temperature of ice causing the ice to melt.)

2) Lemons are sour because they have no sugar. (Lemons have some sugar, just less sugar than oranges.)

3) Oranges are sweet because they have sugar.

4) The sky is blue because all of the other colors get absorbed
by water in the atmosphere. (The sky is actually blue
because of light scattering-- called Raleigh scattering.)

5) Ice cubes float because they repel soda, water, and milk. (Ice
cubes float because ice is less dense than liquid water.)

6) Ice cubes will not float in oil.

7) Ice cubes will float in oil.

8) Thunder is louder when it is closer because the sound hits our
ears sooner and has less chance to go someplace else if
we are close. (Thunder travels as a sound wave. The
further we are from the thunder, the more the sound gets
dampened as it hits molecules in the air during its
travel.)

9) Steel balls and marbles sometimes feel cold in our hands
because they allow heat to exchange and cotton balls do
not allow heat to exchange.

These are some examples of hypotheses. Explain to the students that not
every hypothesis is correct. Explain to the students that when scientists
formulate a hypothesis, they do not already know the correct answers.
A scientist is making an educated guess. The next step in the scientific
method, designing an experiment, will help determine whether or not
the hypothesis is correct.

Explain to the students that because a hypothesis is a guess, a scienti
must do something, like design an experiment, to test whether or not t
hypothesis is correct.

Discuss with the students how the boy in the text tests for whether sa
makes rubber sticky. Help the students think of ways they might test f
sugar in a lemon or test another hypothesis. For example,

1) Lemon juice can be collected and the water evaporated.
Sugar might be visible in the remaining residue.

2) Lemon juice residue could be compared to orange juice
residue.

3) Ice cubes could be placed in several liquids such as water,
milk, soda, and oil to determine if ice cubes always float.

Tell the students that it is sometimes difficult to design experiments, a
not every question can be answered. For example, it may be difficult for
student to design an experiment to test with certain whether or not lemo
have sugar. The residue may contain other chemicals that do not allo
one to say definitively whether or not a lemon has sugar. Also, explain
the students that there is no "one right way" to do an experiment; howev
there are usually certain parts to an experiment that make it better. F
example, controls are used to make sure the experimental setup is workir
properly. Controls can be either positive or negative.

A positive control tells the scientist how the results for an experimer
might look if the hypothesis is true. For example, if lemon juice has suga
and if it is possible to evaporate the water from the lemon juice, then
scientist might want to know what sugar evaporated from water mig

ook like. To find out, a positive control of just sugar and water can be used. The scientist would mix sugar and water together, let it evaporate, and then examine the residue. He could then compare this control with his xperiment and find out if they look similar. If they do, he might conclude hat there is sugar in the lemon juice.

A negative control tells the scientist how the results should not look or if positive control might be confusing. For example, it may not be easy to ell the difference between salt water and sugar water. A scientist might et up a negative control where salt is used instead of sugar. If evaporated alt water looks similar to evaporated sugar water, then it won't be easy to ell if the residue from the lemon juice is sugar or salt. Thus another test is eeded, like tasting the residue.

Once an experiment has been designed, results are collected as the xperiment is carried out. This is the next step in the scientific method. Explain to the students that it is very important that all of the results be ecorded. This includes results that the students did not expect. Sometimes najor scientific discoveries are found by results that were not at all expected. A good scientist has a keen sense of observation and does not let what he xpects to happen determine what he records. Some possible results for emon juice are the following,

1) No residue was found after the water dried.

2) Residue was found.

3) The residue did not taste like anything.

4) The residue tasted salty (or sweet, or sour).

The final step in the scientific method is making a conclusion. In a conclusion the scientist evaluates the results of the experiment and tries to make a statement regarding the hypothesis. For example, if residue was found in lemon juice and the residue tasted sweet, the scientist can conclude that the hypothesis that "lemons have no sugar" may not be correct. At this point, the scientist needs to determine how conclusive the data are and to check the reliability of the experimental setup. It is important that the conclusions be valid and not state something that the data haven't shown.

1.5 Summary

Go over the summary statements with the students. Discuss any questions they might have.

Experiment 1:   It's the law!   Date: _____

Objective: In this experiment we will use the scientific method to determine Newton's first law of motion

Materials:

    tennis ball
    yarn or string (10 ft)
    paper clip
    marble

Experiment:

  Part I

1. Take the tennis ball outside and throw it as far as you can. Observe how the ball travels through the air. Sketch the path of the ball in the space below.

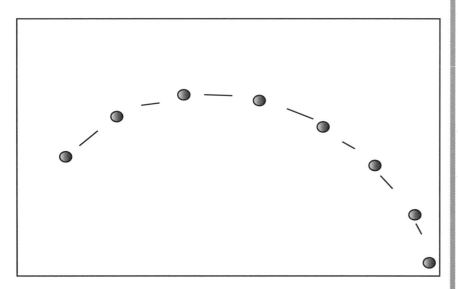

In this experiment the students with discover Newton's first law of motion by observing the motion of a tennis ball and a marble.

Newton's first law of motion is also called the law of inertia. The students will look more carefully at motion and inertia in Chapter 4. However, in this experiment the objective is to show the students that, by observation, they can discover physical laws.

Newton's first law of motion can be stated as follows:

A body will remain at rest or in motion until it is acted on by an outside force.

In the first part of this experiment, the students are to observe how a ball flies through the air. They should notice that the ball will go up and come down in some kind of arc every time they throw it. The arc can be shallow or sharp depending on how they throw it.

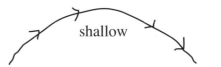
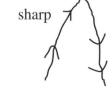

shallow

sharp

Challenge them to throw the ball so that it won't come down.

Ask them if they can get the ball to go up an down in a different pattern, such as,

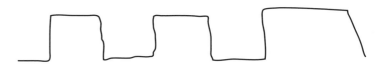

Now, take the string or yarn and attach it to the tennis ball using the paper clip. To do this, open the paper clip up on one side and slightly curve the end as follows:

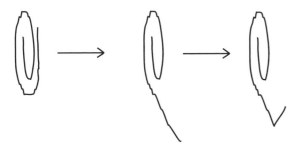

Put the extended curved end of the paper clip into the tennis ball by gently pushing and twisting.

Next, tie the string to the end of the paper clip.

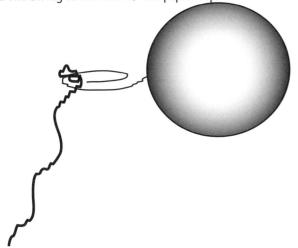

By attaching a string to one end of the ball the students will be able to observe a difference in how the ball will travel once it is thrown.

This is only one way to attach a string to a tennis ball. Several other methods were tried, but it seems that, for us, the paper clip works the best. You may also try a thumbtack or small pin. It is somewhat difficult to puncture the tennis ball with the paperclip, so supervise the students. It might help to put a small hole in the tennis ball with a penknife or ice-pick before inserting the paper clip.

If you do not want to puncture the tennis ball, the string can be wrapped several times around the ball and secured with tape.

5. Holding onto one end of the string, throw the ball again into the air as far as you can. Note how the ball travels, and record what you see in the space below. Do this several times.

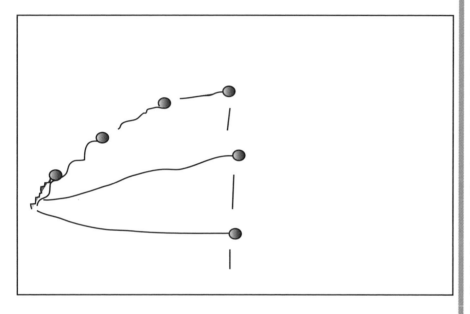

Part II

1. Take the marble and find a straight clear path on the floor or outdoors. Roll the marble on the floor and record how it travels. Note where and how it stops or changes direction. Do this several times and record your observations in the next box.

The trajectory of the tennis ball will now be different. When the students throw the ball, it will begin similarly but when the string has reached its full length, the ball will abruptly stop and fall to the ground.

Have the students throw the ball several times. Ask them if they can change how the ball falls to the ground. They should notice that if they shorten the string, the ball does not travel as far as when the string is longer. They should also notice that, if they do not throw the ball very far and the string does not reach its end, the ball will travel almost as if there is no string attached.

Without telling them the answer, help the students see that the ball's trajectory only changes when the string can act on it.

In Part II, the students will examine how a marble rolls. Have them roll the marble on a smooth surface. They should notice the ball traveling mostly straight. Have them compare this with a ball rolling on a rough surface. Discuss with the students why they think the ball may travel differently.

You can also have the students place obstacles in front of the marble, such as small building blocks. They should be able to observe the marble traveling straight on a smooth surface until it contacts an obstacle.

Again, help the students see that the marble's trajectory is not changed unless it is contacted by something -- like a rough surface or a building block.

smooth surface

rough surface

Conclusions:

_____

_____

_____

_____

_____

_____

_____

_____

Help the students make conclusions based on the data they have collected.

Some possible conclusions are as follows:

1) The tennis ball goes up and always comes down.

2) The string keeps the tennis ball from going all the way up because it pulls the tennis ball back.

3) The marble travels on the smooth surface in a straight line, but the rough surface keeps the marble from traveling straight.

4) The marble changes direction only when it hits a block.

After the students have thought about their data and drawn some conclusions, discuss Newton's first law of motion. Show them how they were able to observe the same things that Newton observed and that they, too, could *discover* a fundamental law of physics.

Review

Define the following:

physics   *the study of how things move and behave in nature*

law   *a precise statement about how things behave*

List the 5 steps of the scientific method

observation

forming a hypothesis

experimentation

collecting results

drawing conclusions

NOTES:

Chapter 2: Force, Energy, and Work

Time Required:

> Text reading - 30 minutes
> Experimental - 1 hour

Experimental setup:

> NONE

Additional Materials:

> Fresh fruit such as a banana, apple, or orange

Overall Objectives:

This chapter will introduce the students to the fundamental concepts of force, energy, and work. These concepts can be difficult to understand. It is not important that the students completely grasp everything about these concepts. This chapter is only a qualitative introduction, and the students should be encouraged to think about them, but not necessarily understand all of their subtleties.

2.1 Introduction

This section introduces the terms "energy", "work", and "force".

Discuss with the students their own ideas about the terms work, energy, and force.

Ask them:

> What is energy?
> Can energy be created or destroyed?
> What happens to the energy in a battery when the battery dies?
> What is work?
> When you move bricks from the front yard to the back yard, is
>   that work?
> Is lifting a book work?
> Is dropping a book work?
> What is force?
> Can you give some examples of force?

Many of their answers may be incorrect, and they may have some misconceptions about energy, work, and force. For example, the energy in a battery is not destroyed when it dies. The usable energy has only been converted into a form that cannot be used any longer. This is a common misconception; students will better understand the nature of energy by examining this misconception.

2.2 Force

This section examines the nature of force in more detail. By definition, a force is something that changes the position, shape, or speed of an object.

Using this definition, discuss with the students some of the forces they experience every day. For example,

> What happens when they jump?
> What happens when they collide with another player on the
>   football field?
> What happens when they lift a heavy object?
> What happens when they drop a heavy object?
> What happens when they pull or push on a door?
> What happens to a marshmallow when they squeeze it?
> What happens to a steel ball when they squeeze it?

Explain to them that forces are acting in all of these examples.

Discuss gravitational force. Gravitational force is an attraction between any two bodies with *mass*.

Mass has two very important roles in physics. First, as in the previous paragraph, any two bodies with mass will attract each other by gravitation

o, the amount of mass determines how strong gravitational forces are. ig objects with large masses attract each other much more than smaller ojects with small masses. The *weight* of any object is the gravitational traction between the object and the earh (as measured at the earth's urface). So, *weight* is a force, not mass. Note that the English unit,(pound) a unit of force, while the metric unit (kilogram) is a unit of mass.

econd, the mass of an object controls its inertia, the tendency of any body resist movement when acted on by a force. A body with a large mass ill accelerate slowly when acted on by a force, but a body with a small ass will accelerate quickly when acted on by the same force. At first lance, this seems like a completely different property than gravitational traction. It is indeed a very strange fact that one property of matter, ass, controls two seemingly different things. The fact that *gravitational ass* and *inertial mass* are the same is called the "equivalence principle." he equivalence principle is the basis for Einstein's theory of gravitation lso called general relativity). Both inertia and gravitation arise from one ing -- the curvature of space itself!

he students will look at inertial mass in more detail in Chapter 4.

he force due to gravity is calculated as follows:

$$F = G * m_1 m_2 / d^2$$

here G is the universal gravitational constant, m_1 is the mass of the first ody, m_2 is the mass of the second body, and d is the distance between the vo bodies. Ve can see from the equation that a body that has more mass will have a reater force. Explain to the students that because their mass is so much

less than the mass of the earth, their gravitational force is much smaller and so they cannot pull the earth towards them. This is why they come back to the earth when they jump rather than the earth shifting upwards to meet them. (Do they think it might be possible to shift the earth by having everyone jump at the same time? Why or why not?)

2.3 Balanced forces

Explain to the students that, when objects aren't moving, forces are balanced.

The most fundamental equation defining force is Newton's third law of motion:

$$F = m \text{ x } a \text{ or } a = F/m$$

where F is force, m is mass, and a is acceleration. This equation says that the force exhibited by an object is equal to its mass multiplied by its acceleration. If the acceleration of an object is zero, then the net force acting on that object is also zero. Conversely, a force acting on an object causes it to accelerate. For a given force, an object of small mass will acclerate more than an object of large mass.

Explain to the students that, in the drawing, a ball is sitting on a shelf. You can see from the diagram that the arrows point in opposite directions. The ball is pushing down on the shelf, but at the same time the shelf is pushing up on the ball. Point out to the students that the forces are equal but acting in opposite directions.

In this case, the ball does not move, so the net force is zero.

F_{net} = [force of the ball pushing down] - [force of the shelf pushing up] = 0.

The forces are balanced, that is, they cancel each other out.

Explain to the students that objects that are moving but not *accelerating* also have balanced forces. Discuss the diagram with the hockey puck and show them that, although the hockey puck is moving, it is not *accelerating*.

2.4 Unbalanced forces

When forces become unbalanced, the object will accelerate. Acceleration is the change of an object's speed over time, like a car speeding up from a stop light or a ball speeding up when it is dropped. An object's speed also changes when it slows down, so slowing down is also a form of acceleration (called negative acceleration or deceleration.) Just as a massive object is hard to speed up, it is also hard to slow down.

Discuss with the students some examples of unbalanced forces:

Does a ball thrown in the air have balanced or unbalanced forces? Why? *Unbalanced, because it speeds up and slows down.*

Does an airplane when it takes off have balanced or unbalanced forces? *Unbalanced, it speeds up to take off.*

Does a car going from a stoplight have balanced or unbalanced forces? *Unbalanced.*

2.5 Work

The concept of work may be difficult to understand because when we hear the word "work," we think of mowing the lawn or doing the laundry. However, in physics, work is defined as follows:

work = distance x force

The illustration in the student text shows that, for the same amount of force, the work a short weightlifter does is less than the work a tall weightlifter does because the distance is less for the short weightlifter.

Discuss with the students other examples relating work, distance, and force. For example,

If you carry a box of books up one flight of stairs and your brother carries the same box up two flights of stairs, who has done more work? (*Your brother.*) How much more work has he done? (*Exactly twice the amount of work.*)

If you carry a box of books up one flight of stairs and your brother carries a box of books that has half the mass up one flight of stairs, who has done more work? (*You have.*) How much more? (*Exactly twice as much.*)

If you push on a concrete wall for an hour and it does not go anywhere, how much work have you done? (None!)

Help the students think of some of their own examples. The more examples they can discuss, the more they will understand the relationship between work, distance, and force.

.6 Energy

nergy is another concept that can be difficult to grasp because when e hear the word "energy," many different ideas come to mind. Energy asically gives objects the ability to do work. The different kinds of energy, uch as potential energy, kinetic energy, and heat energy, will be discussed a more detail in later chapters. What is important for the students at this oint, is for them to begin thinking about where the ability of an object to o work comes from.

sk the students to list some forms of energy that they are familiar with nd discuss what kind of energy they think might be used.

What do you need to make a car run? *gasoline (chemical energy)*
What do you need for a flashlight? *batteries (chemical energy)*
What do you need for a CD player? plug into an outlet *(electrical energy)*
What do you need to carry books up a flight of stairs? *muscles (mechanical energy), food (chemical energy)*

.7 Summary

o over the summary statements with the students. Discuss any questions ey might have.

NOTES:

Experiment 2:   Fruit works?   Date: _____

Objective: _____

_____

Hypothesis: _____

_____

Materials:

slinky
paper clips (2)
apple
lemon or lime
banana
ruler
balance or food scale

Experiment:

1. Try to decide, just by "weighing" each piece of fruit in your hands which piece will do the most work and which piece will do the least work on the spring.

2. State your prediction as the Hypothesis.

3. Now, weigh each piece of fruit on the balance or food scale.

4. Record the weights on the next chart.

In this experiment the students will try to determine how much work a variety of fruit can do. Remind the students that

work = distance x force

Have the students read the entire experiment, and then help them think of possible objectives. For example,

Using a slinky, we will find out if a banana can do more work than an orange.

We will measure the work fruit can do.

We will find out if two bananas do more work than one.

Have the students make a guess about which fruit can do the most work. They should be able to tell just by weighing the fruit in their hands which one is the heaviest. Have them state this for the hypothesis. For example,

A banana is heavier than a lemon and will do more work.

An orange is lighter than the apple and will do less work.

Two bananas will do more work than one banana because two bananas weigh more.

Using a food balance or a small scale, have the students weigh each piece of fruit and record the weights in the chart.

Fruit	Weight (oz. or g)

. Next, take the paper clip and stretch one side out to make a small hook.

. Place the hook in one of the pieces of fruit.

. Hold the slinky up to the level of your chest and allow 10 to 15 coils to hang below. You will have to hold most of the slinky in your hand.

. Measure the distance from the floor to the bottom of the slinky with the tape measure. Record your result below.

istance from floor to slinky _____

. Now place the piece of fruit that has the hook in it on the slinky and allow the slinky to be pulled out by the fruit.

0. Measure from the end of the slinky to the floor with the tape measure and record your results below.

1. Repeat with each piece of fruit. Record your results in the next chart.

After the students have recorded the weights of the fruit, have them use the paper clips to create hooks for the fruit. We found that the paper clips work fairly well, but younger kids may find tape more effective. The fruit can be fixed to the end of the slinky in any manner.

The students will have to experiment with the slinky and number of coils. We found that having the students hold most of the coils in their hands with only a few coils hanging works fairly well. Also, instead of holding the slinky, they can attach it to the branch of a tree or some other fixed ledge. Just make sure the slinky is free to extend and does not contact any other surface.

Have the students first measure the distance from the end of the slinky to the floor without a piece of fruit on it. The distance should be around 2 or 3 feet. Make sure that once this distance is measured, the number of coils allowed to extend is not altered. If the distance is too short (that is, the fruit extends the slinky to the ground), reduce the number of coils used and remeasure the distance to the floor.

Have the students fix the fruit to the last coil in the slinky and allow the coils to extend. Have them measure the distance from the ground to the bottom of the piece of fruit.

Fruit	Distance from floor to slinky	Distance extended

Have the students subtract the distance the slinky extended without fruit from the distance it extended with the fruit on it. This will give the net displacement. Have them record this in the column marked "Distance extended."

11. Subtract the distance you recorded in step 8 from each of the distances you measured and recorded in the previous chart. This gives you the distance each piece of fruit has extended the slinky.

12. Calculate the work each piece of fruit has done. Record your answers in the next chart.

Fruit	Work

Have the students calculate the work each piece of fruit has done. They calculate this using the following equation:

$$work = distance \times force$$

Force is the weight of the fruit.

13. What would happen if you put two pieces of fruit on the slinky? Test your prediction and record your answer in the next chart.

(2)Fruit	Distance from floor	Distance extended	Work

Now, have them predict what would happen if they placed two bananas or two oranges on the slinky. They should predict that two pieces of fruit will do exactly twice the amount of work. Have them test this prediction by fixing two pieces of fruit to the slinky and measuring the distance the slinky extends. Have them record their results.

4. Make some conclusions about your results and record them in the
   Conclusions section.

Conclusions:

_____

_____

_____

_____

_____

_____

_____

Help the students make valid conclusions about their results. Also, help them record any problems they may have encountered. For example,

The banana did more work than the orange.

Two bananas did twice the work of one banana.

Two bananas did not do twice the work of one banana.

The slinky extended too far, and we could not measure two piecees of fruit.

The apple and orange weighed the same and did the same amount of work.

Challenge question:

In the Review there is a challenge question. Have the students think about whether this would be possible, and then help them do a rough calculation.

The mass of the earth is 5.98×10^{24} kg.

The mass of an average human is 66 kg.

According to the US Census, the world population is 6,341,930,833. *http://www.census.gov/cgi-bin/ipc/popclockw*

Total mass of people = # people x mass per person = (6,341,930,833)(66kg) = 418,567,434,978 kg $\approx 4 \times 10^{11}$ kg.

Answer = *NO*-- There are not enough people and they pull in all different directions since they are spread around the earth.

Review

Define the following terms:

force   *something that changes the position, shape, or*
           speed of an object

work   *work = distance x force*

energy   *gives objects the ability to do work*

Circle the correct answer in each pair for the following question:
  Which object has the greater gravitational force?

  a banana or a (bowling ball)
  a (car) or a bicycle
  the moon or the (earth)
  the earth or the (sun)

Answer the following questions:
  Is a book sitting on a shelf doing work?_____*No.*_____
  Is a bowling ball crashing into the pins doing work? *Yes.*___
  How much work is done if you lift a 3-lb box 2 feet? *6 foot-lb*___
  How much work is done if you lift a 2-lb box 3 feet? *6 foot-lb*
List some forms of energy:

  potential energy   *chemical energy*   *electrical energy*

Challenge:
Do you think if we could get every person on the earth to jump all at
once, we could move the earth? Why or why not? Can you do a rough
calculation?

NOTES:

Chapter 3: Potential and Kinetic Energy

Time Required:

    Text reading - 30 minutes
    Experimental - 1 hour

Experimental setup:

    NONE

Additional Materials:

    Banana

Overall Objectives:

In this chapter the students will be introduced to two different types of energy -- *potential energy* and *kinetic energy*. Potential energy is energy that has the potential to do work, and kinetic energy is the energy of motion. The main objective of this chapter is to help the students understand that energy exists in different forms and that it is converted from one form to another. In this chapter students will investigate how potential energy is converted into kinetic energy and vice versa.

3.1 Potential energy

Potential energy is energy that has the potential to do work. Discuss with the students the meaning of the word "potential." Make sure they understand that potential energy is already energy, but that it isn't doing any work. Potential energy has the *potential* to do work. Ask the students to give some examples of potential. For example:

A child has the potential to become a famous scientist.

A seed has the potential to become a plant.

A puppy has the potential to become a dog.

In the text, a book on a table is used as an example of potential energy. Explain to the students that this type of energy is formally called gravitational potential energy.

Gravitational potential energy is abbreviated GPE. GPE is the potential energy of an object that is elevated off the ground.

Discuss with the students that the amount of GPE an object has equal the amount of work that was needed to lift the object in the first place Ask the students the following questions:

In the Review section for Chapter 2, you calculated the work for lifting a 3-lb. box 2 feet. How much GPE does this box have?
6 foot-lbs

In the Review section for Chapter 2, you calculated the work for lifting a 2-lb. box 3 feet. How much GPE does this box have?
6 foot-lbs

3.2 A note about units

When the students calculated work and the GPE for an elevated box they multiplied two numbers with different units. Explain to the students that a unit describes the type of quantity being used. Discuss with the students that there are different kind of units. There are units for weight such as pounds and ounces; units for mass, grams, and kilograms; units for length, such as meters, kilometers, inches, feet, and miles; and units for time, such as seconds, minutes, and hours.

Explain to the students that when they multiplied 3 lb x 2 feet they got a unit of foot-lb. It is an awkward unit from the English system, but it is a unit of energy.

There are two different systems for units in common use. In the United States, most people are still taught the English system of units. Most Americans use the English system for measuring weight, length, and volume. Units in this system are feet, inches, miles, ounces, pounds, etc

preferred system of units for science is the metric system. In the metric system the units are divisible by 10, which makes calculating different quantities easier than with the English system.

etric units include meters for distance, grams for mass, and liters for volume. Discuss the table on page 18 of the student text and show the students the various equivalencies (i.e. how many inches equal a foot, how many feet equal a mile, and so on). Show the students how numbers with metric units are easier to calculate than numbers with the English system. For example,

> How many centimeters are in 5 meters? *(500 -- multiply by 100)*
> How many inches are in 5 yards? *(12 inches/foot, 3 feet/yard =*
> *(12 inches/foot) x (3feet/yard) x 5 yards = 180 inches)*

3 Types of potential energy

section 3.1 the students were introduced to potential energy. Gravitational potential energy is only one kind of potential energy. There are other nds of potential energy, such as chemical potential energy, elastic strain potential energy, and nuclear potential energy, to name a few.

iscuss with the students other kinds of potential energy. For example,

> What kind of potential energy is in cereal? *chemical*

> What kind of potential energy is in a battery? *chemical*

> What kind of potential energy is in a rubber band? *strain* or *mechanical*

> What kind of potential energy is in a spring? *strain* or *mechanical*

3.4 Energy is converted

Discuss with the students how energy gets converted. This is an important fundamental concept that the students should know. Energy is neither created nor destroyed -- only converted to other forms of energy. It is important that the students understand the following:

Potential energy is useful only when it gets converted to another form of energy.

Ask the students if they can find any useful ways to use different kinds of potential energy without converting the energy into another form, such as using batteries for tree ornaments or jewelry.

3.5 Kinetic energy

Explain to the students that the potential energy of the book on the table gets converted into kinetic energy when it moves from the table and begins to fall. Discuss the Greek word root for kinetic, *kinetikos*, which means "putting into motion." Explain that kinetic energy is the energy of motion.

Have the students think of some other objects that have kinetic energy. Ask them if the following things have kinetic energy:

> A car going 45 miles/hour? *Yes.*

> A tennis ball in motion? *Yes.*

> A basketball sitting still on the floor? *No.*

A toddler who is not sleeping? *Yes.*

A parent at the end of the day? *Not always.*

Explain to the students that the kinetic energy of an object depends on two things -- the mass of the object and the speed of the object. The formula for kinetic energy is

$$KE = ½ \, m \, s^2$$

where *m* is the mass and *s* is the speed. Explain to the students that KE is proportional to both the mass of the object and its speed. This means that heavier objects will have more KE at a given speed than lighter objects and slower objects will have less KE at a given mass than faster objects.

Also notice that the KE is proportional to half of the mass and the speed squared. This means that there may be much more kinetic energy in a fast-moving toddler than his slow-moving parent!

3.6 Kinetic energy and work

Recall that work is simply the force of an object multiplied by the distance the object is moved. We know that objects having kinetic energy are moving and that, if they hit another object, they can cause the object they hit to move. There is work done when potential energy is converted into kinetic energy and when kinetic energy is converted into other forms of energy, such as heat and sound. The work done on an object equals the change in kinetic energy of that object.

It is not important for the students to completely grasp this concept, only that, when a moving object contacts another object, energy is converted and work is done.

3.7 Summary

Go over the summary statements with the students. Discuss any question they might have.

Experiment 3:   Smashed banana   Date: _____

Objective: _____

_____

_____

Hypothesis: _____

_____

_____

Materials:

    stiff cardboard
    board (over 3 feet)
    straight pin or tack
    small scale or balance
    small to medium-sized toy car (1)
    one banana sliced
    10 - 20 pennies

Experiment:

1. Read through the laboratory instructions and then write an objective and a hypothesis for this experiment.

2. Take a portion of the cardboard and make a backing to put the sliced bananas on. Fix a sliced piece of banana to the cardboard near the bottom.

3. Make a ramp with the board. The end of the ramp should meet the sliced banana. Your setup should look like the next figure:

In this experiment the students will convert the gravitational potential energy of a small toy car into kinetic energy and do "work" on a banana.

Have the students read the entire experiment and write an objective. For example,

> *We will measure how much GPE is needed to smash a banana.*

> *We will show that a heavier toy car needs less height (less GRE) to smash a banana.*

Next, have the students write an hypothesis. For example,

> *The toy car will not be able to smash the banana no matter how high the ramp.*

> *The toy car will smash the banana when the ramp is two or three feet high.*

> *The toy car does not have enough mass to smash the banana.*

> *The toy car needs to have at least 50 pennies to smash the banana.*

Have the students assemble the apparatus. It helps if the board is smooth and reasonably straight. A cardboard tube, such as a wrapping paper tube, also works if cut lengthwise and opened up to make a trough. The cars should have good wheels and roll smoothly and easily to reduce friction.

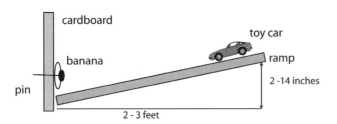

4. Weigh the toy car with the scale or balance. Record your result.

    Weight of toy car (ounces or grams) = _____

5. Place the toy car on the ramp and elevate the ramp 2 inches. Allow the toy car to roll down the ramp and hit the banana. Record your results in the next chart.

6. Elevate the ramp another two inches. Now, the ramp should be 4 inches off the ground. Allow the toy car to roll down the ramp and hit the banana. Record your results in the chart.

7. Repeat with the ramp elevated 6 inches, 8 inches, 12 inches, and 14 inches and record your results in the chart.

We found that we needed to put several pieces of banana at the bottom because the car often does not travel straight.

Have the students weigh the toy car. Small toy cars typically weigh between one and two ounces.

Have the students roll the toy car down the ramp and elevate the ramp in 2-inch increments each time, allowing the car to travel down the ramp and hit the banana. We found that an average toy car does not really smash the banana until the ramp has been elevated over 12 inches.

Height (inches or centimeters)	Results (write your comments)
2 inches (4 centimeters)	
4 inches (8 centimeters)	
6 inches (12 centimeters)	
8 inches (16 centimeters)	
10 inches (20 centimeters)	
12 inches (24 centimeters)	
14 inches (28 centimeters)	

Answer the following question:

1. What happened to the speed of the

    car as the ramp increased   *Speed increased* _____

2. At which ramp height did the banana smash?   _____

Now add 10 pennies with tape to the toy car. Weigh the toy car again and repeat rolling the toy car with the pennies down the ramp with the ramp elevated 2 inches, 4 inches, 6 inches, 8 inches, 12 inches, and 14 inches. Record your results.

Weight of toy car plus 10 pennies (ounces or grams) = _____

Height (inches or centimeters)	Results (write your comments)
2 inches (4 centimeters)	
4 inches (8 centimeters)	
6 inches (12 centimeters)	
8 inches (16 centimeters)	
10 inches (20 centimeters)	
12 inches (24 centimeters)	
14 inches (28 centimeters)	

nswer the following questions:

At which ramp height did the banana smash? _____

. Did the banana smash at the same ramp height for the light car and he heavy car? _____

. If "no" to question 2, which one was higher? _____

Now have the students add pennies to the car to make it heavier. Have the students reweigh the car and repeat the experiment. They should discover that the ramp will not need to be elevated quite as high in order for the toy car to smash the banana.

Using the equation:

gravitational potential energy = weight x height

calculate the GPE for the height that smashes the banana for the toy car with and without the ten pennies. Record your answers below.

GPE for car without pennies _____

GPE for car with pennies   _____

Is the GPE the same [or close to the same] for both cars?_____

Conclusions:

_____

_____

_____

_____

_____

_____

Have the students calculate the GPE for the toy car with and without pennies at the corresponding heights for which the banana was smashed.

The GPEs should be roughly equal. Basically, we expect that it takes a given amount of KE to smash the banana, and it doesn't matter whether this comes in the form of a heavy, slow car or a light, fast car. The energy needed to smash the banana is the GPE the students calculate.

Have the students write conclusions based on the data they have collected.

Review

Define the following terms:

potential energy *energy that has the potential to do work*

gravitational potential energy *the potential enery of an object elevated off the ground*

chemical potential energy *potential energy stored in chemicals*

kinetic energy *the energy of moving objects*

Fill in the blanks

1 foot = *12* inches

1 yard = *3* feet

1 mile = *1760* yards

1 meter = *100* centimeters

1 centimeter = *10* millimeters

1 gram = *0.001* kilograms

NOTES:

_____
_____
_____
_____
_____
_____
_____
_____
_____
_____
_____
_____
_____
_____
_____
_____
_____
_____
_____
_____
_____
_____
_____
_____
_____
_____
_____
_____
_____
_____

Chapter 4: Motion

Time Required:

    Text reading - 30 minutes
    Experimental - 1 hour

Experimental setup:

    NONE

Additional Materials:

    NONE

Overall Objectives:

In this chapter the students will learn about some properties of motion: inertia, friction, and momentum. It is important for the students to understand that an object will remain in a steady, straight line of motion until a force acts on it. (Review Chapter 2, page 9.)

4.1 Motion

Have the students observe or think about objects that move. Ask them why they think objects move. Revisit the experiment in Chapter 1. Ask them what they discovered about objects that move. Have them reread their conclusions. Explain that what they observed in the experiment was Newton's first law of motion which is stated as follows:

> *An object in motion will stay in motion unless acted on by*
> *an outside force, and an object at rest will stay at rest unless*
> *acted on by an outside force.*

Discuss with the students the significance of this statement. Explain that for 2000 years people thought that a moving object had to have a force pushing it. Aristotle thought that this was how objects moved, but he was wrong. Explain that because Aristotle did not feel the movement of the earth, but saw the sun and moon move in the sky, he thought that the earth was the center and that the sun and moon moved around the earth. Discuss the Greek word roots for *geocentric cosmos*.

Have the students look at the drawing of the solar system in the text. Show them where the earth and sun are with respect to each other. Explain to the students that we now know that we live in a *heliocentric cosmos* in which the earth rotates around the sun. Discuss the Greek word roots for this *heliocentric cosmos*. Explain to the students that there were early scientists who challenged

the idea of a geocentric cosmos, but it took 2000 years for people to finally believe that the earth was not the center of the universe. [Look at the lives of Nicholas Copernicus, Tycho Brahe, Galileo Galilei, and Johannes Kepler] Discuss with the students why they think this might happen. Explain to them that there are a lot of different factors that go into science and that, because science is done by scientists, Copernicus, Brahe, Galileo, and Kepler, there are personal biases and pressures that occur. Explain to them that it is sometimes difficult to replace a prevailing scientific theory with a new theory because of these biases and pressures. Explain to the students that this happens even today, and new theories are not readily accepted if they are a major challenge to the dominant paradigm.

4.2 Inertia

Discuss with the students the concept of inertia. Explain that inertia is the tendency of things to resist a change in motion. Ask them what they think this means.

Ask the students if the following objects are easy or hard to move:

> a toy boat floating on water
> a rowboat on water
> a 20-foot motor boat on water
> an ocean liner on water

Explain to the students that in physics, inertia deals with two things: mass and momentum (section 4.5).

The first is the fact that objects with large mass accelerate slowly, when pushed by a force. If you push on a small object with little mass, for example, a toy boat, it accelerates (speeds up) quickly. On the other hand, if you push a larger object, like a good-sized sporting boat, it will eventually begin to move, but you will have to push for a longer time before it accelerates. Explain to the students that they could even move a large-sized ocean liner like the Queen Mary by pushing on it (in the absence of friction), but it would take time. In this case, inertia refers to an object's mass.

4.3 Mass

It is important that the students understand that mass and weight are *different*. Weight is a force. Mass is not. However, by weighing an object you can tell how much mass it has since the more mass an object has, the more it will weigh on earth due to the greater force exerted on it. Explain to the students that without gravity objects do not weigh anything. In space a boulder floats just like a feather. However, the boulder and feather still have mass. The boulder still has more mass than the feather and, as a result, would be harder to move than a feather -- even in space.

4.4 Friction

Discuss with the students that although inertia keeps things moving, objects on earth will eventually stop. Ask them why anything would stop moving: *because a force acts on the object*. Ask them what force is acting on the following objects to make them eventually stop moving (if the object does not bump into something) and ask if they can "see" this force. [Answer - friction]

> a rolling marble
> a hockey puck on ice
> a car out of gas

Discuss with the students that, although they cannot visibly see the force making these objects stop moving, a force is still acting on them. Otherwise they would never slow down or stop. For a marble, there is rolling friction between the floor and the marble; for a hockey puck, there is slight friction between the puck and the ice; for a car most of the friction is within the engine, wheels, and axles. (Again, this is what the first law of motion states.)

Tell the students that this force is friction. Friction occurs when two objects rub against each other. Explain that friction is a force that works in the direction opposite of the direction of motion. Friction is what slows objects down and eventually causes them to stop. Explain that, in the absence of friction, an object would keep moving forever and never stop.

4.5 Momentum

The second aspect of inertia is the fact that objects with large momentum are hard to stop.

Review with the students the concept of inertia. Inertia is the tendency of an object to resist a change in motion. Objects that are stationary want to remain stationary, and objects that are moving want to stay moving. Review the answers to the questions you asked in section 4.2. The two objects on the list that they could stop were a baseball tossed in the air and a basketball thrown to them.

Now ask them if they could stop the following (without feeling pain):

> a baseball hit with a bat
> a basketball shot out of a cannon

o is the answer. Now ask them, *Why*? Have the masses of these two objects changed? *No.* What is different? *The objects are traveling at faster speeds than before.*

Momentum is inertia in motion, that is, mass that is moving. Momentum makes objects hard to stop.

The mathematical equation for momentum is:

momentum = mass x speed

Explain to the students that objects that have large masses will have large momentums. Also, objects with fast speeds will have large momentums.

.6 Summary

Go over the summary statements with the students. Discuss any questions they might have.

NOTES:

Experiment 4:   Moving marbles   Date:

Objective: _____

            _____

Hypothesis: _____

            _____

Materials:

    several glass marbles of different sizes
    steel marbles of different sizes
    cardboard tube (2-3 ft. long)
    scissors
    black marking pen
    ruler
    two stop watches
    letter scale or balance

Experiment:

1. Using the letter scale or balance, weigh each of the marbles, both
    glass and steel. Label the marbles with numbers or letters or note
    their colors so that you can know what each marble weighs. Record
    your results in part "A."

2. Take the cardboard tube and cut it in half lengthwise to make a
    trough. Mark the middle of the tube with the black marking pen.

3. Measure one foot in either direction of the middle mark and make
    two more marks, one on each side.

4. The cardboard tube should now have three marks; one in the middle
    and two on each side, one foot from the middle. The tube will be
    used as a track for the marbles.

Have the students read the entire experiment and write an objective.
Possible objectives are as follows:

We will examine the movement of different marbles.

We will investigate the momentum of different marbles.

We will see what happens when one marble hits another.

We will see if we can move a heavy marble with a light one.

We will see if we can move a light marble with a heavy one.

Have them write a hypothesis. Some examples are the following:

*The small glass marble will not be able to move the steel
marble.*

The small glass marble will be able to move the steel marble.

The small glass marble will stop when it hits the steel marble.

*The small glass marble will not stop when it hits the steel
marble.*

In step 1, the students will weigh the marbles. Remind them that weight
and mass are different and that they will know the mass of the objects.
However, they will be able to tell which objects *have* more mass -- that
is, those that weigh more.

5. Take the marbles and, one by one, roll them down the tube. Notice how each one rolls. Describe how they roll (Do they roll straight? Are they easy to push off with your thumb? Do they pass the marks?) in Results, part "B."

6. Now place a glass marble on the center mark of the tube.

7. Roll a glass marble of the same size toward the marble in the center. Watch the two marbles as they collide. Record your results in Results, part "C."

8. Repeat steps 6 and 7 with different-sized marbles. Record your results in part "D." [For example, try rolling a heavy marble towards a light marble and a light marble towards a heavy marble.]

Have them mark the marbles or note the colors of the marbles so that they will know which marble corresponds to each weight.

Have the students mark the cardboard tube as described in steps 2-4.

In step 5, the students will roll the marbles down the tube and observe how each marble rolls. Have them describe the movement of the marbles in section B of the Results. Some examples are as follows:

The glass marbles move easily down the tube and off the end.

The small steel marbles move easily down the tube.

The large steel marble takes more effort to move down the tube.

They may notice that it takes slightly less effort to push the glass marble than the heavy steel marbles. This is because the larger steel marbles have more inertia than the smaller marbles.

In step 6, they will place a glass marble in the center of the tube. When they roll another small glass marble down the tube, they should watch closely to see what happens. Have them record their observations in part C. For example,

The rolling glass marble hit the other marble and stopped.

The marble that was stopped started moving when it was hit by the rolling glass marble.

Ask the students to observe and answer the following:

Results:

A.

Marble	Weight

B.

_____

_____

_____

_____

C.

_____

_____

_____

_____

When they roll the glass marble slowly, how far does the other move?

When they roll the glass marble fast, how far does the other move?

They should observe a correlation between how much the second marble moves and how fast the first marble travels. In other words -- fast-moving marbles will cause the stationary marble to move further than slow-moving marbles. Have the students observe this several times.

What they are observing is the *conservation of momentum*. In the absence of angular momentum and friction, the total linear momentum of the traveling marble would be transferred to the stationary marble. However because the marble is rolling (and so has angular momentum in addition to linear momentum) and because of friction, the second marble does not pick up quite all of the linear momentum of the first. Despite this the students should be able to observe qualitatively the second marble moving faster when the first marble is traveling faster. This is because the total momentum is conserved or, stays the same.

A better way to illustrate this would be to use an air hockey table. If one is available, try the same experiment with two hockey pucks. The advantages of an air table are first, that the pucks have little friction so momentum is better conserved, and second, that the pucks are not rolling so there is no angular momentum to complicate things.

Have the students use different-sized marbles. Have them roll a light marble towards a heavy marble and a heavy marble towards a light marble. Help them carefully observe what happens. They should observe the scenario shown in the next diagram:

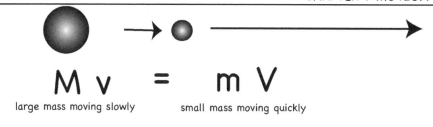

large mass moving slowly   small mass moving quickly

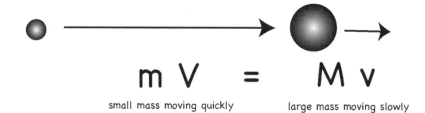

small mass moving quickly   large mass moving slowly

When the light marble impacts the heavy marble, the heavy marble will accelerate only a little bit.

When the heavy marble impacts the light marble, the light marble will accelerate quite a bit.

Have the students repeat this several times. Ask them what they think of these results.

Discuss with them the conservation of momentum. Explain that the total momentum stays the same. Remind them that momentum is mass multiplied by speed. A large mass traveling at a certain speed will cause a smaller mass to have a higher velocity because momentum is conserved. A small mass traveling at a certain speed will cause a large mass to have a lower velocity because momentum is conserved.

Although there is angular momentum in a rolling ball and friction present, the conservation of momentum should be observable qualitatively.

Have the students draw conclusions based on the data they have collected.

Conclusions:

NOTES:

Define the following terms:

inertia *the tendency of things to resist a change in motion*

mass *a property that gives objects inertia*

momentum *a property that makes things hard to stop;*
mass multiplied by velocity or speed

friction *the force experienced by two objects rubbing*
against each other

Write the equation for momentum:

$$momentum = mass \times speed$$

What has more mass: a bowling ball or a green pea? (circle one)

What has more momentum: a rolling bowling ball or a bowling ball shot from a cannon? (circle one)

Chapter 5: Energy of Atoms and Molecules

Time Required:

>   Text reading - 30 minutes
>   Experimental - 1 hour

Experimental setup:

>   NONE

Additional Materials:

>   NONE

Overall Objectives:

In this chapter the students will learn about the energy of atoms and molecules, that is, *chemical potential energy*, Chemical potential energy is found in fuels, foods, and batteries. Students will also be introduced to *nuclear energy*. It is important to help the students note that all of the forms of chemical potential energy are useful only when they get converted to other forms of energy such as light, heat, or electricity.

5.1 Chemical energy

Discuss chemical energy with the students and have them think about different chemical reactions they are familiar with. After reading the text, have them discuss what is happening with the jug, vinegar, and baking soda. Explain to them that, as a chemical reaction occurs in the jug, chemical energy is being *converted* into mechanical and kinetic energy when the cork pops off the top of the jug. Ask them to think of other reactions in which chemiccal energy gets converted into other forms of energy. For example:

gasoline in a lawn mower (chemical to mechanical)

chemical heating pack (chemical to heat)

chemical cooling pack (chemical to heat loss)

chemical light stick (chemical to light)

matches (chemical to heat)

5.2 Stored chemical energy

Discuss with the students the fact that chemical energy starts as chemic potential energy before it is converted into other forms of energy. In the text have the students look closely at a steam engine fueled by wood. Explain, in this illustration, the stored chemical energy in the wood and oxygen gets converted into heat energy when it burns. The heat energy is used to heat water which expands as steam. The work done by the expanding steam is converted into mechanical energy as the piston mo up and down and the train moves forward. In this illustration the energ stored as chemical potential energy is used to convert several different forms of energy from one to another. Have the students look up how c use gasoline and discuss any similarities or differences.

Similarities:

Gasoline is burned to produce heat and expanding gases.
Pistons are used.
The chemical energy in the gasoline and oxygen is converted in Mechanical energy.

Differences:

Water is not heated.
The air in a gasoline engine is compressed.
The gasoline is burned inside the cylinders, not outside.

5.3 Stored chemical energy in food

Discuss with the students that chemical energy is stored in food. Have them look back at Chapter 8 Chemistry, Level I and review the *chemic energy* found in certain foods. Discuss the following foods that have carbohydrates:

potatoes
bread
sugar
spaghetti

plain that the body uses stored chemical energy in foods for energy. e chemical reactions that occur inside the body are complicated, but rall, they amount to essentially the same thing as burning sugar. ny different kinds of reactions take place, but overall, the foods eat get burned and turned into other forms of energy such as heat d mechanical energy (mainly heat). Explain that our bodies require ontinual supply of energy foods because, unlike plants, we cannot duce our own food. Ask them, "What is the one source of energy on ich all plants and animals depend?" *The sun.*

4 Stored chemical energy in batteries

other form of stored chemical energy is found in batteries. Explain t a battery is specifically designed to convert chemical energy into ctrical energy. Ask the students to list items they are familiar with t use batteries. Some examples are as follows:

CD player
flashlight
many different battery-operated toys
automobiles

e first battery was invented by Alessandro Volta. He constructed a taic cell which used alternating layers of metals and salt water to erate electrical energy. The types of batteries used in CD players and hlights are called dry cells. (See Chapter 6.)

A simple battery can be made with a lemon. A lemon, some copper wire, and a paper clip are all that are needed to construct a small battery that can light a small light bulb.

5.5 Nuclear energy

Explain to the students that another form of stored energy in atoms is *nuclear energy*. Nuclear energy is released when the nuclei of atoms split into smaller pieces or when smaller nuclei combine into bigger ones. Explain that nuclear reactions differ significantly from chemical reactions. In nuclear reactions the atoms themselves change their identities (say from C to N); but in chemical reactions the atoms only exchange the atoms to which they are bonded.

Discuss how an atom can change. Explain that, by changing the number of protons in an atom's nucleus, the element changes. Discuss the example showing how a nitrogen atom gets converted into a carbon atom by losing a proton. The carbon atom is called carbon-14 (14 = 6 protons + 8 neutrons). Have the students look on the periodic chart (from Chemistry Level I), and ask them how many protons and neutrons a carbon atom has. Show them that a carbon-14 atom still has 6 protons, but has 8 neutrons--two more than normal carbon. Carbon-14 is called an *isotope* of carbon.

Nuclear reactions release much more energy than chemical reactions. Nuclear energy is used to power nuclear reactors. Explain the design of a nuclear reactor. Show them that the nuclear energy produces heat energy that is used to heat water. The steam from the water turns a turbine that generates electrical energy.

5.6 Summary

Go over the summary statements with the students. Discuss any questions they might have.

NOTES:

xperiment 5:   Power pennies   Date:_____

bjective: _____

_____

ypothesis:_____

_____

Materials:

      10-20 copper pennies
      paper towels
      aluminum foil
      salt water (2-3 T. per cup)
      voltmeter
      plastic-coated copper wire, 4"-6" long
      strong tape (duct tape)

xperiment:

1. Cut out several penny-sized circles from the aluminum foil and paper towel.
2. Soak the paper-towel circles in salt water.
3. Strip off the end of one of the pieces of wire. Tape the exposed metal to a penny.
4. Strip off the end of another piece of wire. Tape the exposed metal to a piece of aluminum foil.
5. Putting the aluminum foil with the wire on the bottom, place one of the wet paper-towel circles on the aluminum foil. Place the penny with the taped wire on top. It should look like this:

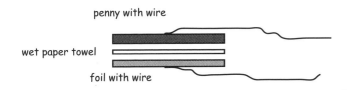

penny with wire

wet paper towel

foil with wire

Have the students read the entire experiment before writing the objective and hypothesis.

Some sample objectives and hypotheses are as follows:

Objective:

To discover how a simple voltaic cell operates.

To construct a voltaic cell and measure voltages.

To see if pennies, aluminum, and salt water can really make electricity.

Hypothesis:

Pennies, aluminum foil, and salt water will not generate electricity.

Pennies, aluminum foil, and salt water will generate electricity.

More layers in the voltaic cell will generate more electricity.

Assemble all of the materials before starting. It helps to scrub the pennies with steel wool. Help the students cut out small, penny-sized circles of aluminum foil and paper. It is important that the cutouts be very close to the size of the penny. Soak the paper circles in the salt water.

6. Take the wires and connect them to the leads of the voltmeter. Switch the voltmeter to "voltage" and record the number. This is the amount of voltage the single-layer battery produces.

7. Add another "cell" to the battery and record the voltage. (A cell is a penny layer, a foil layer, and a paper layer.) It now has two cells. The battery should look like the following:

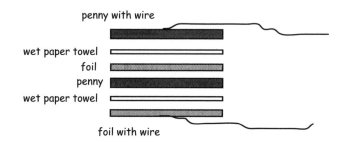

penny with wire
wet paper towel
foil
penny
wet paper towel
foil with wire

8. Continue adding cells of foil, wet paper towels, and pennies, and record the voltage for each newly added cell.

Results:

Cell	Voltage
1	
2	
3	
4	
5	

Help the students carefully strip the plastic off of the wire. It can b difficult to strip just the plastic and not cut the wire itself. The be way is to use a pair of wire cutters or strippers. Gently squeeze an pull the plastic off the end of the wire.

Have the students tape the exposed wire to one penny and one circl of aluminum foil. These will remain as ends. Additional layers will b added in between these two ends.

Next have the students carefully insert one of the salty paper circl between the copper penny and aluminum foil. It helps to set one sid on a firm surface, add the salty paper towel circle, and then place th other side on top, holding it down with your fingers.

Have the students hook the wire leads to a voltmeter and read th voltage. An inexpensive voltmeter can be purchased at any stor which supplies electrical equipment. Carefully read the instruction for the voltmeter. Make sure that the voltmeter is set to "voltage" an that the voltage scale is sensitive enough to detect small voltages. (. typical penny-cell produces about 0.5 V.)

Have the students record the voltage they read on the voltmeter. Nex have them add additional "cells" to the battery. A cell consists of penny layer, a soaked paper layer, and an aluminum layer.

one "cell"

Plot your data. Make a graph with voltage on the x-axis and number of cells on the *y*-axis. Title your graph.

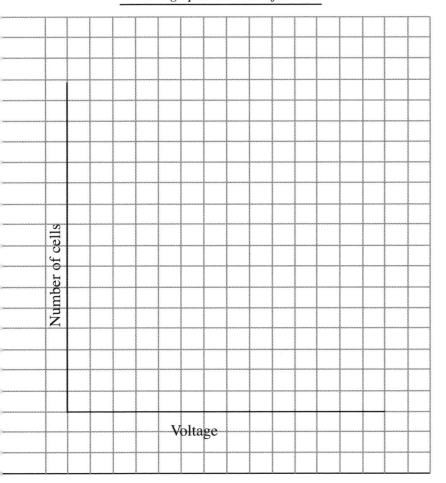

Voltage per number of cells

Have the students record the voltage with each new added cell.

The students should continue to add additional cells and record the voltages for as many cells as they can.

Have the students plot their data. The voltage should be recorded on the *x*-axis and the number of cells on the *y*-axis.

Discuss your data:

_____

_____

_____

_____

_____

_____

_____

_____

_____

_____

_____

Conclusions:

_____

_____

_____

_____

_____

_____

Have the students discuss their data. They should observe that as ﹖ number of cells increases, the voltage increases. However, if there ﹖ places where the paper towel or aluminum foil is larger than the pen﹖ and overlaps and touches a previous layer, there will be a "short." T﹖ electricity will go through the shortest distance. This means that it ﹖ possible to short circuit the battery. If part of one cell touches a previ﹖ cell, one of the two cells will not be counted. If this happens, the volt﹖ will fluctuate. The voltage will appear to increase and then decrea﹖ Have the students discuss these "sources of error."

Paper towels touch.   This cell is "sho﹖ circuited."

Have the students draw conclusions based on the data they ha﹖ collected.

NOTE:

It is also possible to use vinegar instead of salt water. If time permi﹖ have the students repeat the experiment using vinegar, and comp﹖ results with the salt water.

eview

NOTES:

nswer the following questions:

What is chemical energy?

the energy released from chemical reactions

Give two foods that have "food energy" (carbohydrates).

potatoes

pasta

Give two examples of energy we use for fuel.

gasoline (wood, coal, sunlight, etc.)

nuclear reactions

Who made the first battery?

Alessandro Volta

Draw a diagram of a voltaic battery.

penny with wire

wet paper towel

foil with wire

Chapter 6: Electrical Energy and Charge

Time Required:

        Text reading - 30 minutes
        Experimental - 1 hour

Experimental Pre setup:

    NONE

Additional Materials:

    NONE

Overall Objectives:

In this chapter the students will learn about electrical energy. They will review the structure of an atom and examine, in more detail, the nature of electric charge.

6.1 Electrical energy

In Chapter 5 the students were introduced to electrical energy that is produced with batteries. In the experiment for Chapter 5, the students built a voltaic battery and discovered that, as they added more cells, more voltage was produced.

Discuss with the students other types of batteries. The type of battery used in most small electronic equipment is called a "dry cell" battery. Have the students look at some dry cell batteries. DO NOT allow the students to break open a dry cell battery. These batteries contain caustic materials that can burn skin.

Have the students look at different sizes and shapes of dry cell batteries and compare the voltages. Ask them why they sometimes need to put more than one battery in a toy or CD player. Ask them what they notice about how the batteries are positioned in a typical electronic toy.

Ask the students if there are other objects that require electrical energy but that do not use batteries. For example,

    desktop computer
    microwave oven
    washing machine
    hair dryer
    power saw

    electric drill

Ask the students if they are aware of other forms of electrical energy (*static electricity, lightning, etc.*).

6.2 Electric charge

Have the students review the parts of an atom. Review Chemistry Level I, Chapter 2, and explain that the parts of an atom that "carry" electric charges are the electrons and protons. Electrons and protons carry charges, but neutrons have no charge. The "sign" of the charge for protons and electrons (positive or negative) is largely arbitrarily assigned. That is, by convention, electrons are negative and protons are positive. The important aspect is that they are *oppositely* charged.

Explain to the students that

opposite charges attract
and
like charges repel.

Have them look closely at the diagram of the atom. Show that, for a helium atom, there are two electrons and two protons. Explain that the two electrons in a helium atom will try to be as far away as possible from each other. Explain that the positive charges of the protons keep the electrons from flying away from the atom.

6.3 Charging objects

Have the students list some times when they have observed objects being charged. For example,

pulling clothes out of the dryer
rubbing a balloon and sticking it to a wall
dragging their stocking feet on the carpet

Explain that, in any of these cases, objects are being charged by electrons moving from one object to another. Explain that they are seeing charged objects when they observe two objects "sticking" to each other (such as socks coming from a dryer sticking to the bedsheets), or when objects repel each other (such as the individual hairs on their head separating themselves from each other and sticking outward).

6.4 Electric force

Discuss electric force with the students. Explain that electric force is like other forces because electric force causes a change in the shape or speed of something, such as the movement of charged particles like electrons.

Ask the students to list the ways electric forces change the position of an object. Some examples are the following:

A charged balloon will pull objects, such as oppositely charged hair, towards it.

A charged bedsheet will drag a sock out of the dryer.

Plastic packing peanuts become irritatingly charged and are difficult to remove from their container or from anything they touch.

Ask the students if they think they could make a simple instrument tha could detect electric charge. In the experimental section, the students wi construct a simple electroscope where they will detect electric charge.

6.5 Summary

Discuss the summary statements with the students.

periment 6:   Charge it!   Date: _____

bjective:
_____
_____

pothesis:
_____
_____

aterials:

    small glass jar
    aluminum foil
    paper clip
    strong tape (duct tape)
    plastic or rubber rod
    balloon
    silk fabric
    small magnets (2)
    iron filings

periment:

Building an *electroscope* [an instrument that detects electric charge]

1. Cut two thin strips of aluminum foil of equal length (about 1.0" long).

2. Poke a small hole in the
   center of the lid of the
   glass jar.

3. Open one end of the paper
   clip to make a small hook.

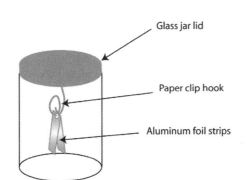

Glass jar lid

Paper clip hook

Aluminum foil strips

Have the students read the experiment and then have them write an objective and a hypothesis.

Some examples are as follows:

Objective:

We will build an instrument to detect electric charge.

We will test for electric charge with an electroscope.

Hypothesis:

Have the students guess what might happen with the electroscope. Give them the hint that the two pieces of aluminum foil will be the same charge. What will the aluminum foil do?

The aluminum foil pieces will separate in the electroscope.

The aluminum foil pieces will stick to each other in the electroscope.

Have the students assemble the parts for the electroscope. Assist the students as they puncture a small hole in the top of the jar.

Have them place the aluminum foil pieces on the paper clip and insert this into the jar.

4. Place the straight piece of the hook through the small hole in the glass jar lid and secure the paper clip to the lid with strong tape. Leave the end exposed.

5. Hang the two strips of aluminum foil from the hook and place it inside the jar.

6. You now have an electroscope.

7. Take the plastic or rubber rod and rub it with the silk fabric, or take the balloon and rub it in your hair or on the cat.

8. Gently touch the balloon or plastic or rubber rod onto the paper clip that is sticking out from the glass lid.

9. Observe the two pieces of aluminum foil and record your results.

Results:
_____
_____
_____
_____
_____
_____
_____
_____
_____
_____
_____
_____
_____
_____

Once the electroscope is assembled, have the students rub a plastic rod (a plastic comb will work) against a silk cloth or in their hair. They should be able to charge the plastic rod.

Have them gently touch the rod to the tip of the paper clip that is sticking out from the jar.

Have them observe what happens to the two aluminum foil pieces. They should see them separate. Have them record what they see. Have them think about the following:

What happens if they touch their fingers to the end of the paper clip?

How long does the charge last?

Are there things that make the aluminum foil separate further? More rubbing? Different plastic rod? A glass rod? A metal rod?

How the electroscope works:

"Like" charges repel, so on a charged object such as a balloon (or the parts of an electroscope), the charges always spread out as far apart as they can. When you touch a charged object such as the plastic rod to the paper clip in the electroscope, the electrons spread from the rod to the clip and aluminum strips. Now the strips both have negative charges, so they repel. After a while the charge leaks away, and the strips come back

Conclusions

_____

_____

_____

_____

_____

_____

_____

_____

_____

_____

_____

_____

_____

together. The bigger the charge, the more the strips repel, so you can tell how strongly charged the rod was to start with.

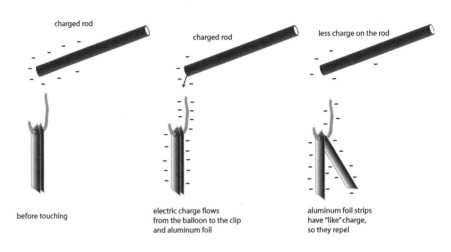

charged rod

before touching

charged rod

electric charge flows from the balloon to the clip and aluminum foil

less charge on the rod

aluminum foil strips have "like" charge, so they repel

Help the students write conclusions based on the data they have collected.

Review

Define the following terms:

dry cell   *batteries that use pastes instead of liquids*

electric charge *the charge assigned to protons and electrons*

electrical force *force resulting from an electric charge*

Circle the correct word to complete the statement:

Like charges ((repel) or attract) each other.

Unlike charges (repel or (attract)) each other.

List the parts of an atom and whether or not they are charged:

proton- positively charged

neutron - no charge

electron - negatively charged

NOTES:

Chapter 7: Moving Electric Charges and Heat

Time Required:

      Text reading - 30 minutes
      Experimental - 1 hour

Experimental setup:

    NONE

Additional Materials:

    NONE

Overall Objectives:

In this chapter the students will learn about electric current, resistance, and heat. It is important for the students to understand that charges move, or flow, through wires as a result of "electric pressure." This "pressure" is the result of a difference in potential (or voltage) in an electric circuit.

7.1 Moving electric charges

Explain to the students that in the last chapter they observed the effects of static charges in the electroscope. Static charges can be transferred from object to object, but once they are in place, static charges do not flow.

Ask the students the following questions:

> How long does it takes for a light to illuminate once the light switch is turned on? (*immediately*)

> How long does it take for the TV to turn on when you plug it in? (*immediately*)

> If you take an extension cord and make the cord very long, how long does it take to turn on the power drill? (*immediately, even with an extension cord*)

> Does the length of the cord matter? (*no*)

Discuss that, when charges move, there is an electric current that behaves much like a hose filled with water. The pressure the water hose experiences when the faucet is turned on causes the water to be pushed out of the hose. In fact, if the hose is completely filled with water, water will immediately flow out the other end. This is similar to how electric current works.

Explain that electric pressure is called voltage. The higher the voltage, the more electric pressure, and the more electrons can be moved.

Explain that wires are made of metals and metals conduct electricity. That is, there are plenty of electrons inside metals that can move. When an electrical pressure is applied to a wire, the electrons inside the wire all move. Explain that this is why the length of the cord does not matter. Electrical pressure at one end pushes electrons out the other end immediately. So the light switch, TV, and power drill all turn on immediately when the cord is plugged into the wall.

Examine with the students the diagram showing several atoms in Section 7.1 of the student textbook. Show them that the electrons move, but the protons and neutrons do not.

7.2 Resistance

Materials that allow electrons to flow easily are called *conductors*. Metals are good conductors because they have lots of electrons that are free to move from atom to atom. Materials that don't allow electrons to move easily from atom to atom are called *insulators*. Insulators are *resistant* to electric flow. Good insulators are plastic, foam, rubber, and cloth.

Electrons can move from atom to atom only if there is a place in the receiving atom to accommodate the incoming electron. Insulators do not have space in their atomic shells to accommodate extra electrons, so electrons do not move.

Explain to the students that in most electrical circuits there are small components called resistors. Resistors are used to slow down the flow of electrons, controlling how much electrical current flows.

ypical resistors look like the following:

he stripes show the resistance value for the resistor.

.3 Heat

hen lots of electric current flows through a wire, the wire often feels arm or hot to the touch.

sk the students to describe some things that are heated electrically. For xample,

> *burners in a stove top*
> *filament in a light bulb*
> *toaster*
> *electric blanket*

sk the students where they think the heat comes from in these cases.

xplain that when electrons flow through a metal, the electrons collide ith the atoms and impart some kinetic energy to the atoms. The atoms ake and vibrate, and we experience this extra energy as heat. The more ectrical current that flows through the metal, the more it is heated. Some aterials get so hot they glow, like a red-hot burner on a stove top or the hite-hot filament in a light bulb.

Have the students list some objects that do not get hot. For example,

> *styrofoam*
> *certain plastics*
> *wood*
> *cloth*

Explain to the students that these are all insulators. They do not conduct electricity, and no electrical current flows through them.

7.4 Summary

Review the summary statements with the students.

Experiment 7:   Let it flow   Date: _____

Objective: _____

_____

Hypothesis: _____

_____

Materials:
    insulated electrical wire
    12 V battery
    some insulating materials (e.g. foam, plastic, cloth)
    small light bulb
    electrical tape
    several small resistors

Experiment:

1. Cut the wire into two foot-long pieces. Carefully shave off the ends of the plastic insulation to expose the metal. Leave about 1/4 to 1/2 inch of exposed metal on each end.

2. Tape one end of one wire to the (+) terminal of the battery. Tape one end of the other wire to the (-) terminal of the battery.

3. Tape the other ends of the two wires to the light bulb. One wire should be taped to the bottom of the bulb, and the other one should be taped to the metal side of the bulb.

4. Record your results.

5. Now place a piece of foam or plastic in between the wire and the bulb.

5. Record your results.

6. Remove one end of the wire from the battery and gently touch it with your finger to see if it is warm.

Have the students read the entire experiment and then write an objecti and a hypothesis. Some examples are as follows:

Objective:

We will find out if materials such as foam or plastic condu electricity.

We will observe electric current and find out what happens if c insulating material interrupts the flow.

Hypothesis:

The insulators will not affect the electric flow.

The insulators will keep the light bulb from lighting.

Materials:

(Optional: Lamp socket and bulb kit # 16020, The Wild Goose)

Have the students carefully strip the plastic off of both ends of the met wire leaving the ends exposed. Then, either tape or wrap the metal wire around the two terminals of the battery.

Next, have them tape the other ends of the wires to a small light bulb. One wire should be taped to the bottom of the bulb and the other should be taped to the metal side. It should look like the following diagram:

7. Record your results.

8. Place a resistor between the light bulb and the battery on one wire. Observe any difference in the intensity of the light bulb. Record your results in the chart. Repeat with two or more resistors.

sults:

	wire only	wire + resistor(s)	wire + insulator
ht bulb ensity			
mperature wire			

swer the following questions about your experiment:

What happened when you connected the battery to the light bulb?

_____

_____

What happened when you put a piece of foam or plastic between the wire and the bulb?

_____

_____

What happend when you put one or more resistors between the light bulb and the battery?

_____

_____

What did the wire feel like to your fingers (with the wire only, with the resistors, and with the insulator)?

_____

_____

Have the students record their results and answer the questions.

They should notice that the light bulb intensity decreases as they add resistors to the circuit. Explain to them that the resistors are behaving like kinks in a water hose. The resistors cut off the flow of electrons like a kink in a hose cuts off the flow of water. The more resistors added to the circuit, the dimmer the light in the bulb will become.

They should also notice that, as more resistors are added, there is less heat in the wire.

When an insulator is placed between the light bulb and battery, students should find that there is no light coming out of the light bulb.

Conclusions:

_____

_____

_____

_____

_____

_____

_____

_____

_____

_____

_____

_____

_____

_____

_____

Have students record their conclusions.

Review

Define the following:

static electricity   *charges that are not moving*

electric current   *charges that are moving*

voltage   *electric pressure*

resistance   *to resist or stand against; a resistor*
resists electric flow

conductor   *material that allows electric flow*

insulator   *material that resists electric flow*

heat   *the transfer of heat energy from one object*
to another because of a difference in
temperature

NOTES:

Chapter 8: Magnets and Electromagnets

Time Required:

     Text reading - 30 minutes
     Experimental - 1 hour

Experimental setup:

     NONE

Additional Materials:

     NONE

Overall Objectives:

In this chapter the students will be introduced to magnets and their properties. Help the students understand that magnetic fields are produced two ways: (1) by spinning electrons and (2) by moving charges (i.e electric currents). The electrons don't hop from one atom to another as in the case of electric current but, instead, spin on their axes. One important concept the students should understand is that electric currents create magnetic fields and magnetic fields can induce electric currents.

1 Magnets

During this reading, it would be helpful for the students to have a few magnets to play with.

Ask the students the following questions:

What happens if one magnet is brought close to another magnet? (*The other magnet will either be attracted or repelled*.)

What happens if you switch the direction of the first magnet? (*Flip it over or use the opposite side? The magnets will do the opposite of what they did in the first question.*)

What happens if you place your magnet near the refrigerator? (*It will stick.*)

Does your magnet stick to aluminum cans? (*No*)

Explain to the students that magnets have *poles* just as the earth has "north" and "south" poles. Poles are not "charged" like the balloon or pieces of aluminum foil from the experiment in Chapter 7, but a pair of poles is much like a pair of opposite charges. They are opposite fields that produce force.

Explain that in a permanent magnet, poles are caused by moving electrons. In a magnet, however the electrons do not move from atom to atom, but stay in one place and *spin*.

Discuss with the students that electrons spin in a magnet much like a basketball can be spun on their finger. The basketball rotates around an axis and can spin in either direction.

All materials have spinning electrons, but not all materials are magnetic. Why? Explain to the students that electrons in all materials spin in both directions. In materials where the atoms share an equal number of electrons, the spins "cancel" each other out and the material is not magnetic. However, in materials where there are an unequal number of electrons spinning, the extra spinning electrons can make the material magnetic. The extra electrons can align themselves and create *poles*.

Explain to the students that the same "rules" apply to magnetic poles that applied to electric charges:

Like poles repel each other.

Unlike poles attract each other.

It is important for the students to understand that, unlike electric charges,

magnetic poles cannot be separated.

If a thin magnet is available that is easy to cut, it would be useful to have the students try to separate the poles by cutting it again and again until it is very small. Each little piece will still have two poles because the atoms themselves are little magnets.

8.2 Magnetic fields

Have the students slowly bring one magnet close to another magnet. If the opposite poles of each magnet are brought close to each other they should experience a pull as the magnet approaches but before the magnets actually touch. Ask them why they think this might be happening?

Explain to the students that the magnets produce magnetic fields that extend out from the magnet into the space around it. A magnetic field affects the space surrounding the magnet. Even though the magnet physically ends at its edges, the magnetic fields extend beyond these physical ends.

There is an easy way to "see" the magnetic fields. If time permits, this simple demonstration should be performed.

Take a magnet and some iron filings. An easy way to collect iron filings is to place a magnet in a plastic bag and drag the plastic bag through some dirt. The iron filings will collect on the outside of the bag. Place the bag and magnet inside another bag and remove the magnet from the inner bag. The iron filings will release from the inner bag and collect inside the outer

bag. Repeat this several times until a teaspoon or so of iron filings ha been collected.

Mix the iron filings with 1/4 cup of corn syrup and pour the mixture int clear shallow dish. (The bottom portion of a clear glass butter dish wo well.) Place the dish on top of a regular-sized magnet. Have the stude observe the iron filings and then wait for an hour and observe them aga The iron filings should align and look similar to the magnetic field li shown in section 8.2.

Explain to the students that the magnetic fields pass through the c syrup without affecting the syrup, but because iron responds to magne fields, the iron filings line up with the magnetic field lines.

Explain to the students that magnets can make other objects temporar magnetic. Using an iron nail, the students can induce a magnetic fi in the nail by having the nail contact the magnet. When the magnet removed, the iron nail will remain magnetic for some time.

8.3 Electromagnets

In the experiment for this chapter the students will build a sm electromagnet. Explain to the students that when an electric curre flows through a wire it creates a magnetic field around it. When a wire coiled, it can behave much like a bar magnet. The more electric curre that passes through the wire, the stronger the electromagnet.

Explain to the students that electromagnets can be quite strong and a often used in junk yards to lift heavy items such as cars. They are a convenient because they can be "turned" off.

NOTES:

4 Electromagnetic induction

plain to the students that a magnet can also cause an electric current flow through a coiled wire. In the experiment for this chapter they ll see how a coiled wire creates magnetic fields, but a magnet can also luce a voltage in a coiled wire. This is called *electromagnetic induction*. raday's law describes electromagnetic induction. Faraday's law is stated follows:

e induced voltage in a coil is proportional to the number of loops times e rate at which the magnetic field changes within those loops.

iis means that the more loops, the greater the voltage; and the faster e magnet is pulled back and forth through the loops, the greater the ltage.

5 Summary

scuss the summary statements with the students.

Experiment 8:   Wrap it up!   Date: _____

Objective: _____

_____

Hypothesis: _____

_____

Materials:

metal rod
electrical wire
paper clips (10-20)
12 V battery
electrical tape

Experiment:

1. Cut the metal wire so that it is one to two feet long.

2. Trim the ends of the wire so that there is 1/4 inch exposed metal.

3. Tape one end of the wire to the (+) terminal of the battery.

4. Tape the other end of the wire to the (-) terminal of the battery.

5. Take the metal rod and touch it to the paper clips. Record your results.

6. Coil the wire around the metal rod. The wire must remain hooked to the battery.

7. Touch the metal rod to the paper clips. Count the coils and record your results.

8. Wrap another 1 to 5 coils around the metal rod.

Have the students read the experiment and then write an objective and hypothesis. Some examples are as follows:

Objective:

In this experiment we will build an electromagnet.

In this experiment we will explore the properties of electromagnets.

Hypothesis:

It won't matter how many coils we use; we won't be able to pick up more than a few paper clips.

The more coils wrapped around the rod, the stronger the electromagnet.

The number of paper clips we pick up will be proportional to the number of coils in the electromagnet.

Have the students assemble the parts for the electromagnet. A screwdriver works well as the metal rod. It should not be magnetized ahead of time. Help the students trim the ends of the wire and fix the ends to the battery. Different-sized batteries can be used, but a big 12 V battery works best. Whenever the wire is connected to both the + and - terminals, the battery is running down; so, don't leave it connected when it is not in use.

Touch the end of the metal rod to the paper clips. Record how many paper clips can be picked up

Continue adding coils to the metal rod and counting the number of paper clips that can be picked up.

Record your results.

Results:

number of coils	number of paper clips

Have the students touch the rod to a pile of paper clips and record the number of paper clips the rod will pick up. Have the students wrap the wire around the metal rod and touch the metal rod to the pile of paper clips.

Have them continue recording the number of paper clips as the number of coils increases.

Using a 12V battery, one student got the following results:

Number of coils	Number of paper clips
10	very weak
15	1
20	2
25	8
30	12
35	15

Your results may vary, but there should be an overall trend that, as the number of coils increases, the number of paper clips the electromagnet can pick up also increases.

Help the students graph their results.

Graph your results below:

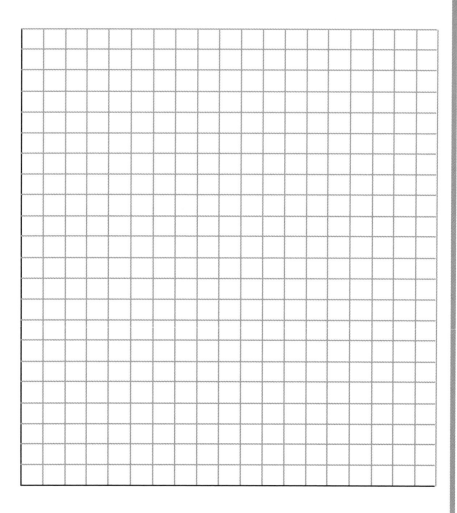

The physics behind an electromagnet:

When a current flows down a wire, a magnetic field is created that ro[...] around the wire:

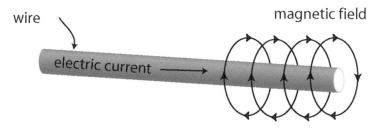

The strength of the magnetic field is proportional to the current; when the[...] is more current, there is a stronger field. If you wind a wire into a coil, t[...] fields from each part of the coil add up to create a net magnetic field th[...] looks much like the field of a bar magnet as shown in the following:

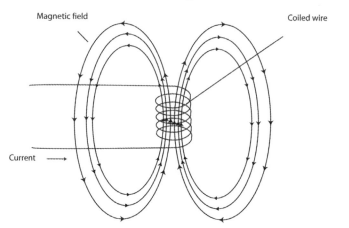

It can be shown that the strength of the magnetic field near the coil[...] proportional to the number of loops in the coil: more loops, stronger fiel[...] So, the students should see a stronger magnet (one that picks up mo[...] paper clips) when (1) the current in the wire increases with a strong[...] battery and (2) the number of loops increases.

Conclusions:

_____

_____

_____

_____

_____

_____

_____

_____

_____

_____

_____

_____

_____

_____

Looking at the graph, help the students discuss their results and draw conclusions based on the data they have collected. Help them discuss any sources of error they might have encountered.

Review

Answer the following questions:

1. What makes materials magnetic?

    an unequal number of spinning electrons

2. Why are some materials magnetic and others not? *Only some materials*
    have an unequal number of electrons spinning.

3. What are poles? *opposite ends of a magnet*

4. Opposite poles (attract) or repel. (Circle the correct word.)

5. Like poles attract or (repel). (Circle the correct word.)

6. What happens if an electric current flows around a metal rod?
    It induces a magnetic field.

7. What happens if a magnetic rod is pushed and pulled through a wire coil?
    It induces a voltage.

Draw a magnetic field.

NOTES:

Chapter 9: Light and Sound

Time Required:

    Text reading - 30 minutes
    Experimental - 1 hour

Experimental setup:

    NONE

Additional Materials:

    NONE

Overall Objectives:

In this chapter the students will be introduced to light and sound energy. They will look closely at waves and their properties, discuss the electromagnetic spectrum and visible light, and examine the difference between light waves and sound waves.

9.1 Light

Ask the students what they think light is. If a flashlight is available, have them explore some properties of light.

What happens to the light when you shine it in the dark? (*It shines in a straight line until it disappears or hits something.*)

What happens to the light when you shine it during the daylight? (*It disappears immediately and you can't see it.*)

What happens if you put your hand in front of the beam? (*the light is blocked*)

What happens if you shine it in a mirror? (*It gets reflected or "bounces back."*)

What happens if you shine it on a nonmirrored surface? (*It disappears into the surface.*)

Can you "catch" the light in your hands? (*No.*)

Can you catch the light in a bottle or a box? (*No.*)

What happens to the light if you close your eyes? (*Nothing. We just can't see it.*)

Can you hear light? (*No.*)

From these observations students should understand that light cannot be "captured," that it bounces back (reflects in a mirror), that it "disappears" in sunlight because it blends into other light, that it can be blocked (by their hands), that it gets absorbed by nonreflective surfaces and that it cannot be detected by other senses -- such as touch or hearing.

Explain to the students that light is actually a combination of electric and magnetic fields. Light is an *electromagnetic wave*. Explain that because light is a wave, it will have the properties of waves. (*Light also has particle-like properties, but this concept is outside the scope of Level I.*)

9.2 Waves

Discuss with the students the nature of waves. Ask them to describe what they know about waves, what waves look like, and how they move. If time permits, have them fill a bowl full of water. Add a small piece of styrofoam or something that will float. With an eye dropper, drop water droplets into the water. Have the students observe how the water moves and how the small floating foam moves. They should see the water "ripple" and appear to bounce off the edges of the bowl and then go back to the center. The small piece of styrofoam will more or less stay in one place. Explain to the students that the water is mainly moving up and down, and the disturbance from the water droplet moves outward.

oking at the drawings in section 9.2, describe the parts of a wave. ow them that a wave has a "peak" and a "valley" and that the peaks are parated by a certain distance called a "wavelength." The height of a ak from the center is called the "amplitude."

ow them that the waves can be stretched or squeezed by moving the aks farther apart or closer together. Explain that this changes the velength, but not the amplitude.

plain that each color of light is an electromagnetic wave with a ferent wavelength. They will look more closely at visible light in the xt section.

plain to the students that we can only see a small part of the ctromagnetic spectrum. Radio waves and microwaves are light, but we nnot see them.

ok carefully at the electromagnetic spectrum and show the students that sible light is between the infrared light and ultraviolet light. Show them at radio waves are much longer than visible light and x-rays are shorter. though we cannot see infrared light, we can often feel it. The heat from ampfire or from a glowing hot burner on a stove is mostly infrared ht being absorbed by our skin and causing it to warm up. Likewise, cannot see ultraviolet light, but it has effects we can detect. UV light m the sun is responsible for sunburns and suntans.

9.3 Visible light

Discuss with the students the different colors of light. For example,

> What are the different colors in a rainbow?
> (*red, orange, yellow, green, blue, violet*)

> Are the colors ever in a different order? (*No*)

> Do you ever see yellow, purple, red and then green in that order in a rainbow? (*No*)

> When does a rainbow occur? (*when it rains*)

> Do rainbows always occur when it rains? (*No*)

Explain that each color of light is at a different wavelength. Show that red is the same as violet, except that the wavelength for red is longer. Explain to the students that by squeezing a red wavelength or stretching a violet wavelength, the light becomes a different color.

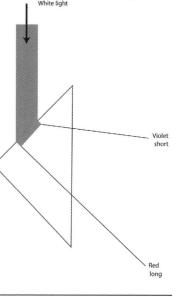

Because colors have different wavelengths, when white light gets split, the colors come out in a particular order. This is why the rainbow always goes from violet to red, red being the longest wavelength and violet being the shortest. A rainbow can A rainbow can be inverted (a double rainbow), but the colors will be in the same order.

9.4 Sound waves

Have the students think about sound. For example, ask them the following:

What makes sounds? (*anything that crashes, birds, musical instruments, etc.*)

If you place your ear on a table and have a friend tap the other end, what do you hear? (*a vibration*)

When you speak, what makes the sound? (*vibrating vocal cords inside your throat*)

What does your throat do as you speak? (*it vibrates*)

Explain to the students that sound waves are not the same as light waves. Sound waves are waves of air particles. When we hear sound, the particles in the air or in a table are vibrating in a wave, and we pick this vibration up with our ears to hear sounds.
Explain to the students that there are different sounds, just like there are different colors. A *frequency* is the number peaks that pass in a given time. Low frequencies have long wavelengths, and high frequencies have short wavelengths. The frequency of sound is called pitch. High pitch means high frequency and short wavelength.

The intensity of a sound depends on its amplitude. Loud sounds have high amplitudes, and soft sounds have low amplitudes.

Discuss with the students the definition of a decibel. Explain that the human ear can be damaged by loud noises. This is why workers in factories and in airports wear earplugs around loud machinery or near airplanes.

9.5 Summary

Discuss the summary statements with the students.

Experiment 9 :   Bending light and circle sounds   Date: _____

Objective: _____

Hypothesis _____

Materials

     two prisms (glass or plastic)
     flashlight
     metal can open at both ends
     aluminum foil
     rubber band
     laser pointer
     long wooden craft stick
     colored pencils
     strong tape (such as duct tape)

Experiment:
Part I: Bending light

Take one prism and shine the flashlight through it at the 90° bend. (See illustration.) Record your results.

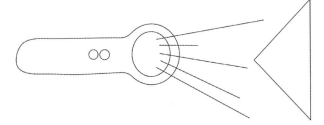

In this experiment the students will examine some properties of light and sound.

Have the students read the entire experiment and then write the objective and hypothesis. Some examples are as follows:

Objective:

> *We will examine light through a prism to separate the colors.*
> *We will look at the wave nature of sound.*

Hypothesis:

> *Sunlight will not separate into different colors through a prism.*
> *Sunlight will separate into different colors through a prism.*
> *The flashlight will not separate into different colors through the prism.*
> *The flashlight will separate into different colors through the prism.*
> *We will see waves with the "sound scope."*
> *We will not see waves with the "sound scope."*

Have the students shine the flashlight through the prism and record the results. Have them take the prism outside and shine sunlight through it. Have them note any differences. This can be tricky to do. Help them angle the prism so that the light will pass through it. The resulting rainbow will be cast ahead of the prism.

2. Now take the prism and shine sunlight through it from the same direction. Record your results.

3. Take the second prism and place it directly in front of the first one, laying it flat on one of the short edges. Using the flashlight, shine light through the two prisms together. (See illustration.)

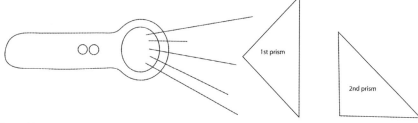

1st prism

2nd prism

Results:

Part I

1. What happens when you shine a flashlight through the prism?

_____

_____

_____

2. What happens when you put the prism in sunlight?

_____

_____

_____

Have the students place two prisms together and shine the flashlight through both of them. Here they will observe a "double rainbow." The first rainbow will have red on the bottom and violet on top (or vice versa depending on how you shine the light through.) The second rainbow will be inverted, that is, exactly opposite of the first rainbow. This can be hard to do, but help the students carefully adjust the angles and positions of the two prisms until the double rainbow is visible. Have them record their results.

raw what you see.

Have the students assemble the sound scope. Make sure the aluminum foil does not become wrinkled.

When working with a laser pointer, have the students be very careful not to shine the beam in their eyes!

The laser beam should reflect off of the aluminum foil and onto an opposing wall. It will usually work best if the laser hits the center of the foil. Have them record what they see as they speak into the can. Have them make both high-pitched and low-pitched sounds.

art II: Circle Sounds

ssemble a "sound scope" in the following way:
 Take the metal can and make sure it is completely open on both ends.
. Place a piece of aluminum foil over one end of the can and secure it with a rubber band. Be careful not to wrinkle the foil; try to keep it smooth.
. Fix the craft stick to the metal can with strong tape.
. Place the laser pointer with the light facing the foil on the craft stick. It should look like the setup in the next diagram.

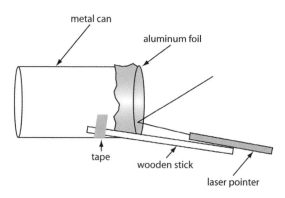

metal can
aluminum foil
tape
wooden stick
laser pointer

Students should observe different-shaped circles. Explain to the student that these are waves. They look like circles because the laser pointer i stationary. If the laser pointer were moving, these circles would look like normal waves. The waves or circles show the vibrations of the aluminum foil, which are caused by the sound vibrations in the air. This experiment allows us to visualize sound.

6. Turn on the laser pointer. (Be careful not to point the laser directly into the eyes!). Observe the reflection on a wall or white board.
7. Holding the can to your mouth, speak into it and watch what happens to the reflected laser light. Record your results.
8. Continue to speak or sing into the can recording as many different shapes as you see.

Draw the shapes you see:

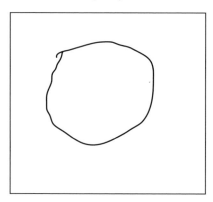

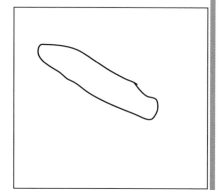

view

fine the following terms:

ctromagnetic wave *magnetic and electric fields combined*

velength *the distance between two peaks*

plitude *the height of a wave from the middle point*

ectromagnetic spectrum *radio waves to gamma rays*

ible light *the part of the electromagnetic spectrum visible to the human eye*

ch *different wavelengths of sound*

equency *the number of peaks that pass over a given time*

e radio waves sound? *No, radio waves are light with long wavelengths.*

NOTES:

Chapter 10: Conservation of Energy

Time Required:

Text reading - 30 minutes
Experimental - 1 hour

Experimental setup:

NONE

Additional Materials:

NONE

verall Objectives:

this chapter the students will connect the various types of energy they ve been studying to learn about the law of conservation of energy. This v states that energy is neither created nor destroyed but is just converted m one form to another. When we hear about an energy "crisis," it eferring to the depletion of usable energy (i.e., energy that can be verted into other forms of energy or work).

1 Introduction

view with the students the types of energy they have studied, and cuss how energy is converted from one form to another.   For example:

gravitational potential energy of the toy car converted into kinetic energy as it rolled down the ramp (Experiment 3).

chemical energy in a battery converted to light energy (Experiment 7)

chemical energy in a battery converted to magnetic energy and mechanical energy (Experiment 8)

electric energy converted into mechanical energy (Experiment 6)

2 Energy is conserved

scuss with the students the drawing showing the toy car travelling wn the ramp. Explain that when the toy car is sitting at the top of the np and is not moving, it has GPE but no KE. Show that, as the car rolls

down the ramp, it picks up KE but loses GPE. Explain to them that it loses GPE because, as it rolls down the ramp, it loses height. As it loses height, it loses GPE. Discuss the equation at the bottom of the graphic. Show the students that, at each point on the ramp, the total energy (which equals GPE + KE) stays the same. Explain that this is what is meant by *conservation* of energy.

10.3 Usable energy

Strictly speaking, in the toy car example, not all of the GPE is converted into KE. Because of friction, some amount of GPE is converted into heat instead. Explain to the students that heat is "unusable" energy. That is, the heat cannot be converted into another form of energy. We say that the energy is "lost," but we really mean it is not useful anymore. Have the students think about other examples where usable energy is "lost." For example,

A light bulb converts electrical energy into light (useful), but it also gets hot (produces heat energy, which is not useful). In the end the electrical energy and light energy are all "gone" -- converted into heat energy.

A car engine converts chemical energy in gasoline into useful mechanical energy, but eventually all of the mechanical energy gets dispersed as heat because of friction (from the air, engine, tires, and brakes). In the end the gasoline is "gone" and the mechanical energy is "gone" too. All of the energy has been converted into heat.

A CD player converts electrical energy into music (useful), but it also produces some heat. In the end the electrical energy is "gone" and can no longer play the music.

Eventually every kind of useful energy gets converted to heat. This is an example of the second law of thermodynamics in action. The energy is not really gone but has been converted into a useless form.

Explain to the students that, when they hear the term "energy crisis," it means that usable energy (energy that can be converted into other forms of energy to do work) is being used up.

10.4 Energy sources

Discuss with the students different sources of energy. Explain to them that some sources of energy, like fossil fuels, cannot be renewed. That is, once they are used they cannot be replaced. Explain that fossil fuels come from plants and animals that died a long time ago. As the plant or animal decomposes, natural gas, oil, and coal get formed. Reservoirs of fossil fuels can be found in between the rock layers under the ground. The fuel can be mined by digging into the ground and removing the fossil fuel. Ask the students to list some fossil fuels and how they are mined.

For example,

coal -- mined from under the ground
natural gas-- found above oil and "mined" or brought to the
  surface with pipes
oil -- pipes are drilled into the ground to remove the oil

Explain that most of the energy we use comes from fossil fuels. Discuss why the fossil fuels will no longer be available some day. Ask the students what we might do when the fossil fuels are gone.

Discuss that there are renewable sources of energy such as solar energy, wind energy, and energy that comes from water. Explain that some of these energy sources are expensive to use right now, but it may be possible someday to use them with greater efficiency instead of fossil fuels.

10.5 Summary

Discuss the summary statements with the students.

periment 10 :   On Your Own   Date: _____

u design this experiment. The goal is to convert as many forms of
ergy as you can into other forms of energy.

r example,

scenario can be designed so that energy is used to put out a fire. A
rble is rolled down a ramp and bumps into a domino with a small cap of
king soda on top of it. A chemical reaction is started when the baking
da falls into the vinegar, which produces carbond dioxide gas that
ts out the fire. In this case the rolling marble has kinetic energy
ich is used to convert gravitational potential energy into kinetic
ergy (the falling baking soda), which then starts a chemical reaction.

Using Energy to Put Out a Fire

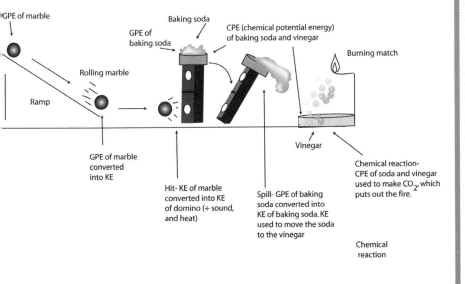

For this chapter the students will design their own experiment. The goal
is to use as many different forms of energy as they can and to convert the
different energies into other forms of energy.

In the example given, the kinetic energy of a rolling marble is used to
knock down a domino that has a cap of baking soda on top. The baking
soda falls into the vinegar and a chemical reaction is started.

In this example, the marble begins with GPE, which gets converted to
KE as it rolls down the ramp. The KE is used to convert the GPE of
the elevated baking soda into KE as it falls. This releases the chemical
potential energy (CPE) in the baking soda and vinegar, and a chemical
reaction starts producing CO_2 which puts out the fire. The chemical
energy is converted into heat energy and bubbles.

Have the students think of ways this example might be extended. For
example, the gas from the chemical reaction could be released into a
small balloon or used to move a small piston.

First have the students do several "thought experiments" by asking
themselves how they might set up a series of small scenarios, like the
example. Some of their ideas will not be practical, but have them use
their imaginations to think of ways to convert energy.

Use the following guide to design your experiment:

1. Write down as many different forms of energy you can think of.

    kinetic energy　　　　　　　　　　　　　　　　　

    　　　　　　　　　　　　　　　　　　　　　　　　

    　　　　　　　　　　　　　　　　　　　　　　　　

    　　　　　　　　　　　　　　　　　　　　　　　　

2. Write down how these forms of energy can be represented.
    kinetic energy

    rolling marble　　*moving toy car*　　*moving ball*　　

Help them narrow some of their ideas into practical applications. Ha[ve] them think of different forms of energy and how they might represe[nt] these different forms.

. Write down ways to connect two or more of these forms of energy.
and explain how one form will be converted into another.

moving toy car bumps into marble and starts it rolling

_____
_____
_____
_____
_____
_____
_____
_____
_____
_____
_____
_____
_____

Next, have them think about ways to link their different ideas. Have them start thinking about whether or not their ideas could work and have them start looking for items that they might use.

. Design an experiment to convert one form of energy into another.
Give your experiment a title and write an objective and a hypothesis.
Write down the materials you need and set up a page to collect your
results. See how many different forms of energy you can convert.
Make careful observations and draw conclusions based on what you
observe.

Experiment 10: _____ Date: ____

Objective: _____
_____

Hypothesis: _____
_____

Materials:

_____   _____   _____
_____   _____   _____
_____   _____   _____

Experiment:

_____
_____
_____
_____
_____
_____
_____
_____
_____
_____
_____
_____
_____
_____
_____
_____
_____

Have the students design their own experiment and write an objective and hypothesis. Help them assemble a materials list and then have them write out the steps of their experiment.

Results:

_____
_____
_____
_____
_____
_____
_____
_____
_____
_____
_____
_____
_____
_____
_____

Conclusions:

_____
_____
_____
_____
_____
_____
_____
_____
_____
_____
_____
_____

Have them record their results, whether or not their experiment worked. Have them write conclusions based on their results and ask them what they might do differently next time.

Extra page (use for graphing or recording more results)

This is an extra page for them to use for recording more results or fo graphing any data they have collected.

Review

Describe the law of conservation of energy

The law that states that total energy is conserved. This means that energy is neither created nor destroyed.

What is the energy that is conserved?

A. kinetic energy

B. potential energy

C. (total energy)

D. chemical energy

What is usable energy?

energy that can be converted into other forms of energy or used to do work.

Name one form of energy that is sometimes unusable.

heat energy or light energy

NOTES:

NOTES:

NOTES: